Shaky Ground

LINDA SHEEHAN

Cataloguing in Publication Data:
Title: Shaky Ground
ISBN 978-0-473-62373-9 (Softcover)
ISBN 978-0-473-62374-6 (ePUB)
ISBN 978-0-473-62375-3 (Kindle)
Subjects: Fiction
Other Authors/Contributors: Sheehan, Linda

Design by initiateagency.com
Revised 2022 edition production by
Castle Publishing Services
www.castlepublishing.co.nz

With thanks to:

The Lord who gave me this gift of writing, and the ability
to put the words in some semblance of order.

Brian Sheehan

Michael & Elspeth Robinson

Christina Cheetham

For all the encouragement to pursue this dream.

One of my favourite verses in the Bible is:

Philippians 4:13 NKJV (New King James Version)

"I can do all things, through Christ who strengthens me"

1

Even though she was awake, her eyes were closed. The dream where she was fighting her way out of somewhere had woken her. The images that had been playing through her mind of a dark night, a car, the noise of a loud bang, now came to the forefront of her mind. In the dream, she screamed, as she realised that she couldn't move. Images of people pulling at her, flashed through her mind. Then the blur of the hospital, someone sticking needles into her and then the bliss of no more pain.

She was lying in a bed, but where she wasn't sure. Opening her eyes, the room didn't look familiar. It was a standard looking room, with a high vaulted ceiling. Gingerly sitting up in the bed, she looked around. The patterned drapes that framed and fell to the floor of a huge window to her left had been pulled open. Then, on the wall in front of her, she could see a door, which was open. Then to the right of that was obviously a wardrobe, with three sliding doors, the middle was a full length mirror.

I wonder why the mirror is covered.

To the right, on the other wall was another door which was shut. There was little furniture in the room apart from the two bedside tables, on either side of the bed; each had a small bedside lamp on it and there was a chair to the right of the closed door.

Twisting her head slightly, she could see the wall behind the bed. There was a huge capital E made of wood going up the wall at an angle, in an elaborate calligraphy script.

Hum!!! My name must start with that. Throwing the covers off, she tested her legs and even though they felt a little stiff, there didn't seem to be any scars on them. There was a bandage on her right arm, shoulder and one around her middle. Sliding towards the left hand beside table, she opened the drawer. *Oh good a bible. I'll look at that later.*

Suddenly the closed door opened and in walked, what was obviously a nurse.

"Good, you're awake." She said, pushing a trolley ahead of her.

"We weren't sure how long you would take to wake up. I know you probably have a lot of questions. We thought that the one that you would most like to know is your name and what happened. On this trolley is some breakfast, if you feel hungry." She then brought the trolley to the left side of the bed. "First, my name is Dee, and yes, I'm a nurse." Putting the tray, that was still covered on the bed.

"Okay, your name is Estelle,"

Estelle, that feels familiar.

"Now your throat may still feel sore, and we suggest that you don't try to speak for the moment, until the doctors can check you out. You can write on this whiteboard, that I brought in." Passing her a white board, a white board pen, and eraser.

"There's a very worried person waiting to see you later. You had suspected spinal injuries, three broken ribs, a broken collar bone, a broken pelvic bone, and a possible broken or cracked sternum. We thought it was better to put you into an induced coma. Then we had to bring you out of the coma slowly and this is the first morning that you have been fully awake."

"How long have I been in a coma?" Estelle wrote.

"Six weeks."

"What happened?"

"That's what the police are still trying to work out."

"The police?"

"Apparently you crashed very heavily into a tree, after your brakes failed. The police also believe that you were rammed from behind, several times."

"Who is waiting to see me?"

"I believe it may be your husband."

"Ethan." Estelle wrote.

"Yes. Now some amnesia is perfectly normal, so that is why we thought it better not to have any photos in here. Do you remember anything?"

"Only fragments."

"Okay, perhaps you can let the doctor know later. Now I suggest that you have some breakfast, then perhaps a shower, and getting dressed." Dee said, sliding all the doors of the wardrobe open.

Estelle could see that it was bigger than she first thought, as Dee walked in.

"How about I hold up a couple of things and you shake your head if you don't like it... Ok."

"Ok" Estelle wrote on the board and held it up for Dee to see and started eating the muesli, and realised that she was indeed hungry.

Four outfits later, she had chosen a very casual loose top and stretch pants, which Dee had hanging on the end of the rack.

"Can I get some more juice?" Estelle wrote.

"Certainly." Putting her head out of the door, Dee, spoke to someone in the hall.

"Now, time for a shower and I have to tell you that there is a mirror in the en suite. It is up to you, if you want to look at your face... It is still quite swollen."

"Am I scarred?" Estelle wrote.

"No."

"Maybe I'll look later; can you cover it for now?"

"Of course. After you are dressed, the doctor would like to see you. Do you feel up to walking? It's not far, but this is your first day horizontal, so to speak, and if you get tired, it would be understandable."

"Is laughing classed as speaking?" Estelle wrote.

"Ethan said that you have a great sense of humour and perhaps laughing in your mind would work for now."

That person looks familiar. Hmm!! She thought, noticing one of the two assistants as she walked into the exam room. *I think she was the one following me, a couple of days before the accident.*

Even after all the tests they thought it best for her not to talk as they explained that, in the accident, she hit her windpipe, thus possibly damaging her voice box. Estelle finally got tired of tapping the whiteboard, where she had written 'When do I get to see Ethan?' As they seemed to be ignoring her.

"My name is Frank Roscoe. I'm the doctor in charge of your treatment. We aren't ignoring you. We have finished all the tests, for the moment. Ethan has been waiting outside. He wants to know if he can come in."

"Yes, of course." She wrote and underlined it several times.

Through the door came three men, the one in the middle was familiar, and in the time that it took them to walk to where she was, several things happened.

Her senses became heightened. She noticed that Ethan was trying to tell her something without speaking. There was a definite warning in his eyes.

I don't think it is normal to have eight people in an exam room. She thought, as her heightened senses kicked into top gear.

"Hi ET" Ethan said, when he got close.

"Ditto." Estelle wrote.

Now, I know that I have to be careful with what I say. She thought.

"Where are the children?" She wrote, knowing that even though they didn't have any children, that this was part of a code that they had worked out. She knew that, his response would also help her with whom she could trust.

"With Uncle Sam & Aunty Diana, in Marton."

That means that the doctor and nurse are safe, but no one else.

"Is Uncle Sam boring them with movies?" She wrote.

"Only some of the silent ones."

So there are cameras, but not all can pick up sound.

"Diana took them to the pools."

No cameras in the bathrooms.

"Must be frustrating, not being able to talk."

"Hopefully not for much longer." Estelle wrote.

"It might for be for longer than you think." The Doctor said quietly.

They want me to stay quiet!

"How long before I get to go home?"

"I want to wait for all test results to come back." Frank replied.

"Ok, What about going outside to get some fresh air?" She wrote underneath four small question marks, as she wanted to know who the goons either side of Ethan were, but couldn't remember the code.

"I gather that Dee told you that some amnesia was expected. Unfortunately, we aren't sure how long this could last. But I assure you, you're quite safe here." Ethan replied.

"I would prefer you to stay inside for another couple of days." Frank said.

"Aunty Diana had to explain to the children about life guards that they saw at the pool." Ethan said.

I know he's trying to tell me about these guys.

"What did she say?" Estelle wrote.

"She said that they were there to protect people."

So these guys are protecting him, now.

It was two days, after she first woke up from the coma that Ethan managed to slip a note to Dee, who then gave it to her, in the shower.

Estelle,

The people following you might have something to do with the case that we are on now. The area in which you crashed is well covered by close circuit cameras and managed to catch the limo that was following you. Even though the license plate was a little blurred, we managed to track it to a diplomat. One camera managed to catch a close up of the driver. It looked like a woman; this probably means that we are getting too close to the 'dirty little secret' of this person. We still don't know why.

I'm going to try to slip another note in with a picture of our supposed children. These are actually a picture of the neighbours grandchildren, Jemima, and Jack. I suspect that the people following us may have figured out that we don't have any children. I am wondering if it is worth continuing with that farce. The doctors and the bodyguards are willing to play along with what we decide. Perhaps a picture of the house or businesses would be better. The police are still investigating the crash and the car is still going through the forensic stage.

I must tell you about the body guards. They approached me the day after the accident and said that they had been assigned to protect us. They said they didn't want to intrude, by staying in the house. I hired a motor home and parked it beside the garage. The electricians dug a small trench for the power cable, from the garage to the motor home, and put up a small connection pole. Maybe, by the time you are allowed to come home, the bit of landscaping I did around it, will have settled.

The body guards never told me their names or explained why the people that hired them felt it necessary to be looking after us.

I know that you would like your laptop to be brought in, but the guards feel that it's not a good idea, as you never know who could have access to it while you are away from it. They also suggested that they could be following any visitors that come here, so Paul, Gina, and Esther decided to stay away for now.

Ethan

I wonder if the case we are working on, and my own search are connected some-how.

Even though Ethan, with the bodyguards, came every day, the next six weeks were filled with her being in the infinity pool, to build up strength. There were more tests as well as other rehab. The most frustrating thing was that she still wasn't allowed to talk, as they wanted the bruising, and swelling on the windpipe to recover, and it seemed to be taking a long time.

2

During her recovery, Estelle was able to reflect. Paul and Gina Barnes told her that she had been abandoned on the doorstep of a nunnery, at the age of three months. The nuns then brought her to the hospital where Gina worked. A note pinned to her explained that her name was Estelle, because of a small birthmark in the shape of an E on her left shoulder blade. Gina and Paul had then adopted Estelle at the age of four months, and added Faith, as her middle name. She grew up in a loving environment, in Pine Hill, Dunedin, with two older brothers, Richard, and Samuel, who were also adopted.

Estelle had always been drawn to reading and watching detective stories. She had always wondered who her birth mother was and why she had abandoned her. The Barnes encouraged her in all her pursuits of her goal to become a detective slash lawyer.

After six months of her pretending take photos, around the beauty salon, which Gina owned, at the age of seven, the Barnes brought her a camera. Her talent for taking photos developed quickly and now there were now several family photos that she had set up and taken. Estelle was always asking if she had any natural siblings to which Gina would reply that she didn't really know.

At the age of eighteen, she attended University, where she was taking classes to help become a better lawyer, detective and photographer. It was in the law classes where she met Ethan. It was also around that time, that she became a Christian.

If we hadn't been seated alphabetically by first names; I wouldn't have met Ethan. Estelle pondered.

Over lunch, they talked.

"Ethan Thorne." He said, introducing himself.

"Estelle Barnes,"

"When is your birthday?"

"April fourth, Nineteen, eighty-eight."

"April second the same year. I'm older by two days." Ethan remarked laughing. "As well as wanting to be a detective, I'm a qualified carpenter."

"Really. I was adopted by Paul and Gina Barnes."

"I'm also adopted and knew that I had been adopted at birth by Mark & Michelle Thorne. They were killed in a horrific car accident last year,"

"Sorry to hear that."

"Thank you. It was while I was going through their effects after the funeral that I found my birth certificate. This told me my birthmother's name, Layla Johns."

"That's good."

"Yeah, I want to find why she adopted me out, about my father, and whether I have any siblings."

"That could be interesting. Want me to help?"

"I'm not sure." Ethan said hesitantly. "Sure, why not. Two heads are better than one."

"And a fresh pair of eyes, couldn't hurt."

"That's true."

"I also want to let you know that I'm a Christian." Estelle commented.

"Believe it or not, me too."

"I started off in Sunday School at the local Baptist, church."

"That's where I go to. I'm surprised that I haven't seen you there."

"I'm not able to go every week, because of work commitments."

"Neither am I, but I know that God understands." Ethan replied.

"Do you believe that you were called into being a carpenter, as well being a detective?"

"Absolutely."

It was on their second date that Ethan showed her his carpentry shop, where he made furniture.

Even by being slightly flamboyant in dress, Estelle had this ability to blend in with the crowd. One assignment, in the detective class was to describe their fellow classmates. Neither of them had trouble with this, as they both remembered things other people would take for granted. However, what surprised them most was the way the others described them. Apart from the flamboyancy of her clothes, most of their classmates described both as nondescript.

"This university must have a rule about seating people by their first names." Estelle said leaning over to a girl sitting beside her, while waiting for the first photography class to start.

"They do." She replied.

"How do you know that?"

"It's on the bottom of the enrolment forms. Esther's the name, photography might be my game." She replied.

"I didn't even look there." Estelle giggled. "My name is Estelle. Esther's a pretty name."

"So is yours. Aren't you dating Ethan Thorne?"

"Yes, but how did you know?"

"It is a small campus, and word gets around."

"True." Estelle laughed.

"It could get confusing, with all our first names beginning with E." Esther commented.

"We will be the three Amigos."

"More like the three Emigos." Estelle giggled.

"When's your birthday?"

"April fourth, Nineteen, eighty-eight."

"Same as mine. What's your full name?" Estelle asked.

"Esther Diana Ralph."

"Estelle Faith Barnes."

"Nice to meet you Estelle Faith Barnes." Esther said, hugging her.

They got on so well that they decided to go on photographic assignments together. Estelle discovered that Esther was a Christian as well.

Ethan and Estelle were married by the time they all had finished university, two years later. It was their first client that established their reputation. It didn't take long to prove that the company, for which this client worked, had stolen her idea, for which she had a patent. The company settled out of court, with a multimillion dollar compensation pay out, to the client. The client insisted on paying them a thirty percent commission of three million, which allowed them to start looking for a section on which to build their house and both businesses.

They brought two cars, a Ute with a canopy a sedan, with personalized plates, saying Thorne1and Thorne2. Estelle would often use the Ute to carry the equipment required for the outdoor photography sessions. They also put fifty thousand dollars each into two different term investments that turned over at different times automatically, with the interest going into a savings account.

They rented while looking for the section in an area that they liked. It was while out walking, that they discovered by accident a huge double section, overlooking Sullivan Reservoir, with fantastic views of the mountains.

Both the house and workshop would be the half round barn style, and almost three storeys. The builders took eight months, instead of the usual six, because they built Ethan's workshop first. Ethan was then able to make custom made furniture, for the house. The house itself was huge and had plenty of space for guests and activities and was placed to make the most of the views.

"How did you choose this design?" Gina asked when they were showing her and Paul the plans of the house, before starting the build.

"We both liked it." Estelle replied, shrugging her shoulders.

"I find it a little ironic."

"Why?" Ethan asked.

"Estelle, do you remember the toy farm that you had as a child?"

"Sort of."

"Do you remember the barn that was a part of that set?"

"Yes! I remember I used to play with that a lot, whatever happened to it?"

"I think it got put aside when you became interested in photography. For awhile, though, you did take a lot of photos of barns."

"I had forgotten about them."

"At one stage, we wondered whether our last name had anything to do with your slight obsession with barns."

"Possibly" Estelle laughed.

Ethan and Estelle often worked on cases together and bounced ideas off each other on how the pieces could fit. They also discovered that they didn't really use the offices of the agency much, as they tended to invite clients into the house. They therefore redesigned it and turned into one big space with plenty of cabinets for both photographic and agency records, and moved the reception area to the right, at the end. They had a range of pictures that the photography clients could choose from, that they were able to put up, via a projector, on one of the walls.

Estelle invited Esther to the house, to discuss what to call the photographic business when she asked Esther to join her.

"How about E Shots?" Estelle asked.

"Not sure I like that. It could be either Two Emigos, or E & E Photography."

"I think I prefer E & E Photography." Estelle commented.

"Me too."

Ethan then made a letterbox, out of wood. He burned the business names into it, Thorne Carpentry, Thorne Detective Agency, E & E Photography, and added Three Emigos, down the bottom. A lot of visitors thought that he had spelt Emigos wrong, but once they met Estelle and Esther, they understood.

With the help of Esther, they always tried to keep the set up of the shoot as simple as possible, and often used some of the landscape around the house, and always had the studio available if the weather turned nasty on the day of the shot. They worked well together and would often push each other in their area of weakness, especially in photography. It often came down to a game of rock, paper, scissors, before the client arrived on the day of the shoot, as to who would be actually taking the photos.

They discovered quite by chance, that Julie, the secretary that came in, for up to four hours a day, was good at doing make up, when the makeup artist that Estelle had booked, that day, didn't turn up.

Estelle preferred families, and couples to that of models. One model was so pleased with the shots that Esther had taken of her, for her portfolio that she had then recommended them to her model friends. It was good that there wasn't a stream of models lining up, as the shoots often proved to be very high maintenance and stressful.

Even though, Layla Johns had not named his father, on the birth certificate. They managed to find Ethan's half brother, Zack Johns, who was eighteen months older, within a year of being married. They were still searching for any records regarding Ethan's father and whether he had any other siblings. With neither of her brothers or Zack married, Estelle enjoyed being spoilt by all the men around her, even if it did get a little overwhelming, sometimes.

Both had their own established group of friends and they often had bible studies at the house. It was at one of these gatherings that, Esther met Zack and they started seeing each other. Estelle's brother Richard would often drop in unannounced, to stay. Estelle remarked that it was good that they had extra bedrooms, with Samuel, and Zack often staying.

Ethan and Estelle worked well together, when on cases, they didn't really go for any disguises and where possible Estelle would use her name or a variation of it.

They had been all over New Zealand in order to catch up with some suspects, and kept records of all cases, including the ones that came to them via the police, which could take them as far as Australia, America and England.

Both Ethan and Estelle were qualified lawyers, and detectives. This gave them access to a lot of information that was not normally available. This included birth, and marriage records. They were able to just ring, with a name and then receive by post or fax, the relevant information. This proved invaluable when they were called upon to be part of a court case, as lawyers. Julie was good at organization so that all appointments for the businesses would be typed up on a schedule for two weeks ahead.

They found they were in demand as detectives, because they were known for their discretion. There were the usual clients that thought their husband or wife was cheating on them. Often it would turn out that the husband or wife was actually organizing a surprise birthday or holiday for them. By openly taking photographs out in the public, of a suspect, they would often get shots that could be used, in court.

Esther became the model for some of the photos that were taken on assignment. They had made up laminated, cards saying, that they were taking photos and for any reason, if anyone would prefer not to be in the background of these, to please contact. With the name, address, and phone number, of the business and gave them to each person in the area.

A husband, who thought that his wife was having an affair, had asked them to take photographs. The wife tried to say in court that she didn't know that the photos were being taken. They were able to prove with pictures that Esther had taken with Estelle handing the card to this woman that she had indeed known.

They had been married and running their businesses for ten years now, and both were rethinking their decision, not to have any children.

Estelle wanted to go home and be able to talk to Ethan, freely, without the code as she knew that the house was bug free, but also knew that she would have to bide her time.

Estelle was missing being able to see her parents, but the person that she missed most was Esther.

3

Ethan was able to get another note into Estelle, a couple of weeks into rehab.

Estelle,

The police discovered that the brakes on the car had been cut, probably a couple of days before the accident. As we often swap cars, this means that the accident could have been intended for either of us.

I know that you are very aware of how much I love and care for you, but as you know I'm not into flowery sentiments and this includes this sort of thing. So I thought that I would stick to the facts.

I knew that you would want your bible so that you could have something familiar in the room. I made that E, for you shortly after the accident, and of course we are taking it home with us.

I have a name of the owners of the car. A diplomat named Jacob Blake or Balke, and Co owner Faye Fredricks. I somehow don't think she was the driver, that night of the accident. There are also other names that keep popping up, and as yet I'm not sure where they fit in. Felicity Broadmire and the initials B.J or J.B.

Maybe we can check all this out once you get home.

Ethan

Even after six weeks of the rehabilitation, she was still no closer to being able to speak. The doctor was concerned that there could be permanent damage as the swelling still hadn't gone down. He said that voice paralysis could be the result of damage done by the accident and that the voice could take up to a year to return. With promises to restrict speaking and ongoing appointments set up for a speech therapist, the doctor agreed to Estelle going home at the close of the seventh week.

"It's not going to be easy to bounce ideas off each other, if I'm not allowed to speak." Estelle wrote on the whiteboard, the morning she was going home.

"We'll think of something." Ethan answered. "There's no rush, to brainstorm."

"True, but I would like a few people to be there for this one," she wrote, as they packed up everything and then with one of the bodyguards driving their car, and the other following in a car behind, they drove home.

"Who and any particular reason?"

"My parents, Esther, and perhaps Zack. I think that it is all connected."

"Okay. It was probably good that we don't have any other cases now."

"True, what about any photography sessions?"

"Esther has been taking charge of them."

"Hope she hasn't forgotten to charge and take some commission for herself?" Estelle wrote and added hehehehe.

"She has been getting her commission." Ethan laughed. "After a bit of investigation, I requested all info on Faye Fredricks, Felicity Broadmire, and Jacob Blake or Balke, as well as Blake Jacob."

"Could be one in the same person, using different names." Estelle wrote.

"Could be. The individual I spoke to said that there was quite a bit, so she was going to box it all up. With only two hospitals within a fifty-mile radius of the nunnery. I also asked for all birth certificates that were registered on the same day as yours and my birthday, and within a two-year range. That was about three days ago, so it should be arriving soon," Ethan commented.

"Good thinking." Estelle wrote. And then quickly wiped that off and wrote, "Have you been busy in the workshop?"

"Yes. I have almost ten projects, all in various stages of completion. Now that you are home, I'll be able to spend more time on them."

"You didn't have to spend all the time at the hospital with me."

"I know, but I wanted to be there."

"Aw, that's one of the nicest and the sweetest thing you could of said." Estelle wrote.

"Must be getting mushy in my old age." He remarked, turning and giving her the goofy smile.

"Goof." She wrote, and laughed, softly.

"You know how I had been advertising for someone to join me in the carpentry business."

"Aw. Here I was thinking that you were going to get all romantic on me."

"Perhaps later." Ethan said, blushing, "Back to the question at hand."

"Yes." She wrote.

"A couple of weeks ago a man called Simon Wood started. He is such a natural that I am able to allow him to do work unsupervised."

"That's good."

"I also approached the college to see if they were interested in apprenticeships for carpentry, that I could teach."

"Good idea."

"I was thinking that perhaps once the bodyguards leave that Simon could live in the motor home."

"Any special reason?" Estelle wrote.

"Apparently he is renting about thirty miles away and is finding it difficult to get to our place, as he has no means of transport."

"I don't have a problem with that. I'm finding this not being able to talk interesting."

"In what way?"

"It makes me stop and think about what I want to say, and not to waste words, on what I might be thinking, but not necessarily wanting to say."

"How is that going to work when we do the brainstorming?"

"What do you mean?" She wrote as they arrived at home and unloaded.

"I don't know about you. But when we are brainstorming I have often found that something you have said without thinking will often trigger something in me and make things click."

"Hadn't thought about that aspect."

"Oh well. I have been giving some thought about how we could do a brainstorming session without you talking too much. Remember the movie screen that can be pulled down, that we had installed?"

"Yes, I remember."

"Okay, well, I wondered if I could get a friend of mine to check out whether it is possible to get your laptop connected to that and you type on there, and it appears on the screen, and we could use the screen as a big white board."

"That's brilliant. What about being able to clean it?"

"Let's not get ahead of ourselves; I don't even know whether it is even plausible."

"How do I speak to you, if you are out in the workshop, seeing how I can't use the intercom system at the moment?"

"You could always text me, but I can't guarantee that I'll see it straight away. Let's not make an issue out of a solvable problem."

"That's fair enough."

"My concern is how you are going to indicate to your photography clients."

"Easy, Esther and I think alike."

"True. Don't you go and see the speech therapist, tomorrow?"

"Day after, I was thinking about all this information that could be arriving." Estelle wrote.

"What if we just sort it by names for a start and then read through each pile."

"I thought Julie and Esther could help."

"Good idea, but let's wait and see how much arrives first."

"Okay. Are you available to take me to my appointment?"

"Unfortunately not. Do you think that you could drive?"

"Not sure. Still feel a little shaky from the accident; Maybe Gina could come with me, just in case."

"Do you want me to ring her?"

"I can text her."

"Okay."

Paul and Gina turned up to take Estelle to the appointment, the next morning.

"I didn't think that I would be able to read anything you wrote on the whiteboard and drive at the same time." Gina explained.

Estelle was intrigued when Gina grabbed the whiteboard, on the way home from the appointment.

"Can I talk to you about something?" Gina wrote.

"Sure."

"I would rather come to your place."

"Okay."

"Dad knows what it is all about, but I would rather talk to you in private and I have some things to show you."

"Sounds intriguing."

"More interesting than intriguing."

Estelle was able to report back to Ethan that even though the voice sounded croaky, the therapist was happy with Estelle's progress. The therapist gave her some exercises and showed her how not to strain the voice and suggested she only do three short periods of talking, and stretch that period each day.

A client that Esther had set up, before Estelle came home from the hospital, rang to say that she was unable to keep her appointment set for the following day. She explained she had a broken leg, and arm and couldn't drive. She therefore requested that they both come to her house.

Esther's forte was to make and compile notes for each client. Even with the notes, Estelle could see that this was an unusual one. The client's name was Kylie Simmons and had asked if it was possible to compile a collage of photos of houses that she and her children had lived in over the years.

When they arrived at the rather impressive mansion, Esther explained about Estelle's voice and how she could use the laptop to communicate. Estelle was surprised though, when Esther introduced herself as Diana.

"I became a widow, recently, for the second time. I had two wonderful marriages." Kylie explained.

"Sorry for your lose." Esther said.

"Becoming a widow again has prompted me to do the collage."

"Do you have any address of these houses?" Was the first question that Estelle wrote on the laptop, and then turned it around for Kylie to see.

"Yes, and I would like them to be in order with dates underneath."

"The dates could be added, later." Esther commented.

"There are quite a few addresses."

"Are the people who live there now okay with us taking photos?" Esther asked.

"Yes, but I do want something a little more than just the outside.

"Sounds intriguing." Estelle wrote.

"With each photo of the outside, I would like a compilation of the rooms."

"That's possible."

"Are they okay with that?" Esther asked.

"I wrote to all of them and listed the rooms to be photographed."

"Okay."

"Now there are a couple of other things. I'm not that technically minded and wondered if it's at all possible I could add small pictures of my children, to the houses in order which they were born."

"Possible. Anything else?" Esther asked.

"Yes, I realize that these houses are quite a distance apart and in various cities around the world. I am prepared to pay any expenses incurred in travelling. I would like to know if this can be done within the next six months to a year."

"Possibly." Esther commented.

"I'm willing to pay more than double your usual charges and more if completed early."

"Can we let you know later this arvo or by tomorrow at the latest." Estelle wrote.

"I'll wait to hear from you."

"That was different." Estelle wrote, when they arrived home.

"Sure was."

"Why did you introduce yourself as Diana?"

"Not absolutely sure. Maybe it had something to do with the look that she gave us when we arrived." Esther said, shrugging.

"Okay. Let's look at the addresses."

"And so that you know, I don't have much on my schedule."

"You sound snippy, is everything okay?" Estelle wrote.

"Yes and no."

"Okay. You know that you didn't have to give up your time while I was laid up."

"I know." Esther sighed. "I haven't been feeling well lately."

"Why didn't you say, and have you been to a doctor?"

"I thought that you had enough to deal with, and no I haven't seen a doctor yet."

"I thought you liked being a partner?"

"I do. But you also know that I only do up to five hours a day, and only three days a week."

"Now, I feel stink that I have never asked, what else you do."

"I qualified as a kindergarten teacher, and can get called on, at short notice. That was before I discovered that I like photography better. I am not sure how it will work with what Kylie Simmons wants."

"She did say that she was prepared to pay any expenses."

"True."

"I would also like you to make an appointment to see a doctor and I'll come with you."

"That would be nice. I'm a little scared about what might be wrong."

"Ring now. The sooner we get this sorted the better. I'm sure your employers will understand. If they don't, then resign."

"I quite like it when you take control."

"Yeah, that's me, Miss Bossy boots." Estelle wrote.

"Okay, have rung and made an appointment with the doctor for tomorrow, at two o'clock. You were right, my employers didn't understand, so I resigned." Esther said ten minutes later, coming back into the lounge.

"Good. I know that it is an imposition, but would it alright if you come and picked me up?"

"I took the liberty of texting Gina and asking her to come and do that, and then I."

"Is she available?"

"Yes. Now let's look at these addresses."

"Now, I know she asked us to do them in order, but I wonder if she would be agreeable to doing furthest away first."

"Possibly, and remember I already explained that we can alter any dates later."

"True, and if we set it up so that we have up to a week in each of the places named, it might not take more than a month or two."

"I was thinking that perhaps we could have an extra person come with us." Esther commented.

"Have you thought who?"

"Not yet. I was wondering about your security."

"Ethan said that the bodyguards had approached him the other day and said that their employer had said that any threat to us had now been alleviated, and they would be leaving tomorrow." Estelle typed on the laptop.

"Okay, I wonder what that means."

"Ethan said that they didn't explain that bit."

"Oh well." Esther said, shrugging her shoulders. "Can't be important. I'll be so pleased when your voice comes back."

"Me too."

"This is the slowest conversation that we have had. Waiting for what you type to come up, is excruciatingly slow."

"The therapist suggested that I can only talk softy at this point. I'm only up to ten minutes right now. So, might have to continue this way. Not sure whether it would be any better if you watched what I type."

"Probably not. I have had a sudden inspiration."

"You know, of course, that the sudden inspirations often are the Lord's prompting. Come on, share."

"How about we ask if Gina if she would like to come?" Esther asked.

"What a great idea. That would be nice. Then we need to itemize, the equipment required for the client and explain the idea about the extra person and perhaps ask for a rental van in each place."

"Good idea. Would you like me to ring Gina?"

"Perhaps we can leave booking the flights until we know whether Gina is coming." Estelle wrote.

"How will Ethan feel about you going away?"

"He would probably feel better knowing that Gina could be going."

"If we allow for a couple of weeks to organize schedules, etc., then we could be ready to go away by the end of next month."

"And back by October. Even with allowing a week in each place, it would still a bit of a hectic schedule."

"Would Gina be okay with that?"

"We'll find out tomorrow."

"I'll go and ring Gina, and then ring Kylie and explain." Esther said, going into the agency.

I think Esther is right. This form of communicating is slow. I texted Ethan, more than two hours ago, with all the info and still no replies. Oh well, he should be coming in for tea soon. Wonder if Esther wants to stay?

"All done. Kylie said whatever we need is okay with her." Esther said ten minutes later.

"What about Gina?"

"She'll let us know tomorrow, when she picks us up."

"Would you like to stay for tea?"

"Have a prior engagement with Zack, but I'll see you tomorrow."

"Okay."

"It is certainly nice to know that you don't have anything worse than a virus." Estelle wrote on the laptop, on their way home, the following day.

"Yes" Esther replied.

"I was wondering if you two are busy tomorrow." Gina asked.

"Shouldn't take long to organize flights etc."

"Don't tell me you have changed your mind about coming?" Estelle typed.

"No way. But before we go I would like to show you what I was talking about the other week."

"What's this got to do with me?" Esther asked as they arrived at the house.

"Did you know that you were born in the same hospital as Estelle, and only three minutes apart?"

"We knew that we were born on the same day." Esther commented.

"But not the closeness." Estelle added.

4

The next day, an oblong box, about four feet long, two feet wide and two feet high, arrived via a courier.

"This is going to take longer than I thought." Ethan commented, while waiting for, Gina, to arrive.

"Sure is." Estelle typed and sighed, as they stood in the living room.

"We definitely need some more people to help." Ethan commented.

"True. But it doesn't have to be all sorted before Estelle and I go away." Esther said.

"That's true."

"I think that this is going to take a rethink of this particular brainstorming session." Estelle typed.

"I have been giving that some thought." Ethan commented.

"Don't keep us in suspense."

"You don't have any sessions booked in until well after November, right."

"Right." Estelle typed.

"Hear me out before making any comments okay."

"Okay."

Estelle found big thumbs up and put that up on her laptop.

"I thought putting them in piles by name for a start. I have turned the longest wall, in the photography studio, into one big, long whiteboard. It is three feet off the ground and goes about six feet up. I measured an A4 paper and put A-Z along the bottom of the whiteboard. All of this means that we should have enough room with three trestle tables underneath. We then would be able to stick photos, if any, with their names and any info underneath, and we will be able to draw lines that connect where appropriate."

"I like. That way you could just do as much as you want each day."

"I would rather that we don't do anything but sort it into name piles for now."

"How about we start alphabetically by last name?" Estelle typed.

"And seeing how we are only looking for the last names beginning with, the letters B, F, J, and T, it shouldn't take too long." Esther remarked.

"Good thinking. We each take a small pile out of the box, and so that we are not getting in each other's way, the 'A's start from the left side of the studio. Let's go." Ethan said, picking up the box.

With music going in the background, it wasn't surprising that they didn't hear Gina arrive.

"Time for a break." Gina said switching off the music.

"Yay. I think that we have got quite a bit achieved in an hour." Esther commented, looking at the piles on the tables.

"True, but we haven't even got through a third of the box yet." Estelle typed.

"Baby steps." Ethan commented.

Estelle kept staring at the small box that Gina had brought in, while they ate lunch.

"How busy are you Ethan?" Gina asked as he was about to go.

"Why?"

"I think that you should hear and see what I'm going to show the girls."

"And we do need to also finalize the details of the trip. Maybe Ethan needs to be here for that as well." Estelle wrote on the laptop.

"Good thinking." Esther commented.

"Okay," he replied, shrugging his shoulders. "I'll just go and tell Simon that he's on his own for the rest of the afternoon."

"Now, I can see that you are all curious." Gina said as Ethan came back into the living room. "I have taken the liberty of putting some note pads and pens out and that way you can write any questions down as I explain."

"I have several before we even start." Esther remarked.

"When I was younger, I volunteered as a receptionist at a maternity hospital. The nurses used to tease me about keeping a copy of the records of the weight, length, any distinguishing marks, of the babies, and the initials of the mother. Looking up the records I found that I was on duty on the night you were both born and the night that Estelle was dropped off."

"On the night that Estelle was left, I had come back from my tea break, to discover a Moses basket with a baby girl wrapped in a very expensive shawl had been left there. I still have that shawl. There was a note from the nuns explaining about the birthmark and name and that they had found her on the doorstep of the nunnery earlier that day. Knowing that they couldn't keep her, they had brought her to the hospital."

"Now, I know that Esther wasn't adopted, but I did remember that she was wrapped in the same sort of shawl. Back then, some of the mothers wanted to remain anonymous. There were also quite a few births that night, but only two within the time frame. In both admittance forms were the initials F.F, and F.B. However, we did insist on all visitors putting their name and relationships to the patient in the visitor's book. Besides the relationship, of both those initials was mother. And apart from the first initial K, the signature was totally illegible."

"Intriguing. Can't wait to see how this all ties in." Ethan said. "With the info that Gina just gave us, you realize that you could be in this too, Esther."

"Yes."

"Gina? Is there any record of two girls or perhaps even twins being born the night that both Esther and I were born?" Estelle typed.

"Not sure, I'll have to check. My records are at home."

"Are you thinking that we might be twins?" Esther asked.

"It's within the realms of possibilities. I have noticed that you both have the same sort of mannerisms." Gina commented.

"Let's wait and see, what comes up in the files. Now, for the details of this trip." Estelle wrote on her laptop.

"What, no questions?" Gina asked.

"Not really." Estelle wrote.

"You answered mine already." Esther replied.

"Mum, I must have learnt my organizing skills off you." Estelle wrote.

"How so?"

"I think I know what Estelle is talking about." Ethan replied.

"Do tell?"

"I have been teasing her about the amount of food that she's been cooking and freezing. I guess Simon and I want starve."

"Just ring Paul if you do run out." Gina laughed. "I organized for some friends to be on speed dial."

"Good thing we have a housekeeper that comes in twice a week." Estelle wrote.

"Good old Mrs Peterson. I can tell when she has been, even though I don't know when she comes." Ethan remarked.

"Back to the job on hand." Esther said.

"Sudden inspiration. Esther, what was your mother's maiden name?"Ethan asked.

"Broadmire."

I wonder if Esther is more connected than we thought. Estelle thought.

"So, she will definitely be in amongst the papers. Gina, Esther, I took the liberty of charging two extra laptops up." Ethan said.

"Thank you." They both said.

"I have actually done a bit of homework. I looked at the first four addresses and saw that they were within a hundred mile radius. With the option of a G.P.S system in the rental, this should make it easier." Esther commented.

"Now do you want to stay in a self service place or a hotel?" Ethan said.

"Makes sense to stay at a hotel, and then we don't have to worry about food." Estelle wrote.

"They would take care of the laundry, etc." Gina remarked.

"We could even ask if they could make us a lunch to take with us" Esther said.

"How many days would you need at each location?" Ethan asked.

"Possibly two, but it depends on how long it takes to get there. The outside shots could be dependent on weather, but we are taking the equipment that could help with that as well."

"What if we split that area into two?" Gina asked.

"That makes sense."

"Have you actually goggled all those addresses?" Gina asked after Esther handed them each a copy.

"No."

"I think that you'll find that the Cambridge and Hamilton addresses mentioned are actually in New Zealand."

"Really!" Esther commented.

Now, how am I going to get Ethan's attention? Thought Estelle. *Still not allowed to talk for too long and definately not allowed to shout. I don't want to worry him, but I needed to ask about the other day. I know Esther and Gina don't know about the security guards we had. If I put hi E.T. on the subject he should realize not to read all of it out. Do you still have a contact number for those security guards? I want you to check out whether it was them outside of the house.* Explaining what she saw.

"Estelle wonders why, a van has been parked just down the road for the past week?" Ethan read out.

"I had noticed it and thought that the power or some other company were working the area." Esther commented.

"How about I ring all the utility companies and ask." Gina said.

"Can I ask a favour?" Esther asked.

"Sure."

"I was wondering if I could stay here. My landlord wants to fumigate my place, to help get rid of the cockroaches." Esther squirmed. "He is also talking about putting the rent up."

"When does he want you out?" Ethan asked.

"Within the next week. I thought that he wasn't going to do the fumigation until next month, but apparently the cockroaches have increased recently." Esther replied squirming again.

"Of course, you can stay here." Estelle typed. "You could have the closest bedroom. Would you like help with moving?"

"The house I was renting was partially furnished, so I don't have much."

"How about you move tomorrow and that way you'll be here before we have to leave." Estelle commented.

"That sounds a good idea." Esther answered.

"I managed to check with the security guys." Ethan said, later after Esther and Gina had left.

"I didn't think you had their number."

"I had forgotten that they gave me a number before they left."

"So what did they say?"

"They had been asked to keep an eye on us again for the week."

"Did they say why?"

"Apparently they were asked to take photos of the people coming and going."

"Really!"

5

Estelle had gotten up early, turned the fire up, that she had left going the night before and was now sitting, in the studio with her feet up on another chair, staring at the whiteboard.

We started this case last June. I know the puzzle is all there, but the pieces don't fit. She thought as she reached for the coffee. *We left here in August of this year and were only away two months. It was nice that the three of us managed to fit going to church several times.*

"Can't you sleep either?" Esther asked as she came in with a couple of chairs and set them up the same. "Don't answer that until I come back, must grab a coffee. Wont be long."

"Kylie's photos are ready to be delivered." Esther commented when she came back.

"Good. Something about her request, is really bugging me." Estelle said softly.

"Me too. What is your time limit for being able to speak up to now?"

"About an hour and a half."

"Oh good. Remember how she said that she wanted us to add the photos of her children."

"Yes?"

"I got an email the other day saying that she had changed her mind." Esther said.

"Really!"

"She didn't even give me the names of her children either. Said to add the dates in order and that would be fine."

"Did you inform her that your name isn't Diana?"

"Didn't see any point. Did you see the look Kylie gave us?"

"Yes, she looked as though she had seen a ghost."

"Even some of the people, whose houses we photographed, looked at us funny too. The whole trip went quicker than I thought, though" Estelle commented.

"That was probably due to Gina's organizational skills."

"True." Estelle said, smiling.

"She had everything timed, almost down to the minute."

"I'm used to it."

"You might be. And even though I like getting up early. To have my work out timed was a bit much."

"Oh come on. It wasn't that bad."

"True. And I did come back fitter." Esther said, laughing.

"It was really nice that Gina organized the tours of some of the churches in the areas, over in England."

"Especially St Paul's."

"Yes, and to be able to go to a service there." Estelle sighed.

"I know what you mean. Even though we don't get much chance to attend church here because of commitments, I know that God is pleased, with us."

"True. This is so slow, and frustrating."

"No pain, no gain."

"Very funny." Estelle laughed.

"How are you and Zack getting on?"

"He asked me to marry him the other day."

"Congratulations. So when is the wedding?"

"We haven't chosen a date. We have been looking to build and found a double section, just down the road. We thought that we would start building before we set the date."

"Wow."

"Even when we started going out we set some boundaries."

"What do you mean?"

"Strange as it seems these days, we are both virgins and wanted to wait. Because he often stays here, he was the one that suggested that he would take the room furthest away."

"Aw. How romantic."

"Have you found out whether Ethan and Zack have any siblings?"

"No siblings. An hour to go."

"Did Gina give you her records?"

"Yes, but I haven't had a chance to look at them." Estelle commented.

"Where are they?"

"The two journals that look like books on the other end of the trestles."

"You have one, and I'll have one." Esther suggested.

"Have you got your birth certificate with you?" Estelle asked after five minutes.

"Sure, I'll go get it."

"Okay." Estelle said, when Esther had returned. "Take a look at this" Pointing to the page in question. "There were only six girls born that night. Now the initials F.F and F.B appear to be around the time in question. F.F had a girl, which is recorded as a stillborn. However, mum records her leaving with a girl, a couple of days later."

"Do you think that she may have had twins, and one was the stillborn?"

"Possibly, but that would have been recorded."

"True."

"Now, this is where it gets confusing. F.B and we know that that could be your mum, is recorded as having twins, but leaving with only one. Do you think that someone could have altered either of those initials?"

"It wouldn't take much." Esther said, standing up at the whiteboard and demonstrating.

"Mum recorded that the distinguishing marks on the two girls were the same. An E shaped birthmark. One had it on her left shoulder and the other..."

"Her right shoulder." Esther finished, pulling her top across her shoulder, and turned to show her.

"So we are those twins." Estelle said, showing her left shoulder.

"And I'm the older one." Esther sighed.

"I have this feeling that Kylie is connected too."

"Me too. That could mean that Kylie could be our grandmother." Estelle said.

"Yes."

"Do you remember meeting your aunt?"Estelle asked.

"No. But, I do remember Mum mentioning the name Faye."

"Did your mom ever talk about her or Kylie?"

"No, and I don't remember seeing any photos."

"Strange. Where's Zack today?"

"Gone to the section. The architect is meeting him there."

"Why aren't you there?"

"He said I'd be bored and that I should be here. Where's Ethan?"

"In the workshop. Got up about an hour after me. He popped in here, on his way through."

"I have half an hour of talking left. Your parents are still alive right?" Estelle said after five minutes of them both staring at the whiteboard."

"Yes. Mum and Dad separated when I was twelve. I decided that I wanted to live with dad, and that put a strain on the relationship between myself and mum. Dad had a major stroke five years ago. He now lives in a care facility. I find it hard to visit, as he has really deteriorated." Esther said, wiping away the tears.

"You already know that I have two adopted brothers. Do you have any siblings?"

"An older brother."

"Here, I was hoping for a sister."

"Instead, you get another brother."

"I'm happy with that, and that I found you."

"Aw shucks."

"What's your brothers' name?"Estelle asked.

"Roman."

"Where is he?"

"He disappeared five years ago."

"Around the same time as your Dad had the stroke."

"Yes. Roman and Dad were having this very heated argument, just before Dad's stroke."

"Did they argue a lot?"

"Not really. The thing is I think that Roman blames himself for causing the stroke."

"Strokes can happen anytime."

"True. With Dad so unwell, who do I get to walk me down the aisle?"

"No uncles?"

"Not that I know of."

"Can't be that hard to find a Roman Ralph."

"I think that he may have changed his name or going by his middle name Michael."

"Maybe we can tempt him out of hiding with the offer to walk you down the aisle."

"I hadn't thought of that."

"When's his birthday?"

"June thirtieth, nineteen eighty six."

"Do you have a photo?"

"Here on my phone." Showing Estelle.

"Send it to me. Apart from having plastic surgery, he wouldn't have changed that much."

"Done. Do you think that you can find him?"

"We have contacts, outside the norm, so to speak."

"Are they legal?"

"Of course. Have you talked to your Mum lately?"

"No, not really. I sent her an email telling her about being a partner in a photographic business. I also told her about the trip, and that I was now boarding with my business partner and her husband without mentioning any names."

"Did she reply?"

"Yes, and that's what I feel a little guilty about. She said that she had forgiven me for the decision that I made and would leave it up to me to get in contact. To be honest, what with moving, and the trip, I haven't had a chance."

"Does she know about Zack, the engagement, or your house?"

"No. Okay, what do you have in mind?"

"Why don't we have a dinner?" Estelle suggested.

"I like. We could invite all of the parents without saying why."

"I want to know, when we have to deliver the photos to Kylie."

"Three weeks time, why?"

"I think we have a lot of questions for Kylie. I was just thinking that it might be better to have a meeting with Kylie first, then have the get together to celebrate your engagement."

"You're probably right." Esther said, sighing. "I think I hear the boys talking in the workshop. Shall we go tell them?"

"I would love to help you tell them, but my time is up for today, but I can certainly join you."

"I'll do all the talking."

"Funny, but I can't do much about it at the moment."

It was quite amusing watching the reactions of both men as Esther explained. First Ethan congratulated them on their engagement. Then the look, of shock they shared, when Estelle showed them the entry in the journal and they both showed their birthmarks.

"I knew that you two were more than just friends." Ethan commented, embracing Estelle.

"Me too." Zack said, embracing Esther. "These two are pretty special.

6

"Zack and I have an appointment with the architect. Are you able to take Estelle to the speech therapist later?" Esther asked a couple of mornings later.

"Of course." Ethan replied.

"What's that folder in your hands?" Estelle wrote on her whiteboard.

"It's a collage of pictures of bits of houses that both Zack and I like." Esther said, showing them. "We're hoping that the architect will be able to incorporate some of them into the design we have chosen."

"Are both of you happy with the choice?" Ethan asked.

"Not really."

"If he's any good. He'll be able to draw up something totally new and unique, from these photos." Estelle wrote.

"What a brilliant idea. I said that I would meet Zack at the architect office."

"He should be able to draw it up today." Ethan said.

"By the way. I left a message on Kylie's phone, yesterday, that we are ready to deliver her photos, on Friday of next week. I had a reply this morning." Esther said.

"What did she say?" Estelle wrote.

"Said that she was leaving for on holiday that Friday and wondered if she could come and pick them up earlier that week."

"Have you answered her yet?"

"No."

"Reply that Tuesday afternoon about two o'clock would be better."

"That way we all hear the answers. Like it." Esther commented.

"Me too." Ethan said, giving them both a high five.

"I have enough time before meeting Zack to fire off that email and text now." Esther commented.

The therapist offered the use of a room in her offices, after the examination, and explaining the results of the tests.

"Are you happy with the results?" Ethan asked.

"At least I don't have to start all over again," Estelle said softly.

"And it will only take a week to build back up to the two and half hours."

"True. Go through the three options again."

"One, talk for ten-minute periods, several times a day, and up to the two-hour limit. Two, talk for twenty minute period, the same time limit. Three, talk for the two hour period,"

"I think I prefer the last one."

"Why not add the one day off as well?" Ethan asked.

"Could do."

"Shall we go home, or would you like to go and have afternoon tea somewhere?"

"Sounds good. Good thing you know what I like."

"Why?"

"Because my throat is starting to feel sore."

"Would you rather we went home?"

"No. We haven't had a lot of time together lately."

"Remind me to pick up the gargle solution that the therapist suggested."

"Will do."

"You two look as though you had a good afternoon." Esther commented as they came into the lounge, much later.

"We certainly did. We got some coffees and sat in the park." Ethan remarked.

"How did the appointment go?"

"I haven't done any major damage. I picked up a viral infection. Have to drop back to two hours of talking a day and then build it back up by five minutes a day. Have some options on how I do that. Also picked up an antibacterial gargle which I use twice a day. The only reason, I am writing this on the laptop, is that my throat is sore, and I decided that this day is my day for not talking." Estelle wrote.

"Perhaps some ice cream could help." Ethan suggested.

"Good idea. Want some Ethan?" Esther asked.

"No thanks."

"I'm really pleased that it is nothing more, than a sore throat." Esther exclaimed as she gathered two bowls, spoons and the ice cream.

"Do you two have the twin thing where you can feel if something is wrong with the other or finish each other sentences?" Ethan asked.

"Not that I know of. What about you Estelle?"

Estelle shrugged her shoulders and shook her head.

"Why do you ask?"

"I know that I haven't had much time to brainstorm or even look at the whiteboard."

"You have got a lot of work on."

"True." Ethan said, sighing. "Esther, I really appreciate that you have been able to work on this case."

"Thank you. I started night classes shortly after I joined Estelle in the photographic business. It's taken longer, but I'm now a fully qualified detective."

"Why didn't you tell us?" Estelle wrote.

"I wanted to surprise you."

"Well, it is certainly a surprise, but a nice one. Congratulations." Ethan said.

"Would you like to be a partner in the Agency?" Estelle wrote.

"Of course, as long you don't change the name. The Thorne Detective Agency has a very good reputation."

"Ok." Estelle wrote.

"I know Estelle's just dying to know how you got on with the architect." Ethan commented.

Estelle punched Ethan's arm playfully.

"You were right. After seeing the pictures, he asked us about the style of house we wanted. He then started drawing as we were talking. It was amazing to see it come to life. Then he gave us a copy after drawing it up. I put it in my room, I'll show you later. By the way I played a little bit of phone tag with Kylie."

"She uses a lot of technology for someone that says that they don't understand it." Ethan commented.

"Maybe she understands a lot more than she says." Estelle wrote.

"Could do. The upshot is that she can make it on the Tuesday."

"That works in well." Estelle wrote.

"Have you received any information regarding Roman, Faye or Kiri?"

"There are some emails in my in box, which I haven't had a chance to check. Let's look together." Estelle wrote, opening the email.

"Looks like Roman lives in Australia." Ethan commented.

"Darwin to be exact."

"Estelle, I know that you can't have the email open at the same time as well as wanting to make any comments. Shall I grab the white board?" Ethan asked.

Estelle nodded.

"Then you can write any comments or questions on there." Esther commented as Ethan went to fetch it. "Shall we wait until Ethan comes back?"

Estelle nodded.

"I finally found it. Not sure what it was doing in the car." Ethan explained coming back after a good twenty minutes.

"I think I left it there." Estelle wrote on the board.

"That's one mystery solved." Ethan remarked.

"We decided to wait for you to return." Estelle wrote.

"Good. Open the email up again. Right, we already know he lives in Darwin."

"And he hasn't changed his name or anything." Esther commented.

"Roman is engaged to Rachel."

"Open the attachment." Ethan said.

"Ethan, is your laptop close?" Esther asked.

"Yes, over there."

"Are you on Facebook?"

"I use Estelle's page mostly."

"What's up?" Estelle wrote.

"You're not going to believe this. I've seen these photos. They were posted on one of my friend's page."

"Shouldn't take long to find him on there then."

"Have just sent him a message via my friends' page. I explained that I had been looking for him."

"Wonder what he does for a living?" Ethan asked.

"I guess we will find out."

"Good." Ethan remarked. "Will it be your talking or rest day, when Kylie comes?"

"Rest day." Estelle wrote in reply.

"Perhaps we should charge up all the laptops. I plan to be taking notes." Esther remarked.

"Good idea."

"Who should greet Kylie at the door?" Estelle wrote.

"Might have to me." Esther replied.

"Sorted." Ethan remarked. "Any other emails?"

"Two." Esther answered.

"Let's look." Estelle wrote.

"This says that Faye could be using the name Broadmire."

"Even though Faye was spotted in Darwin, our friend knows that she doesn't live there, and thinks that she could live in Sydney. Our friend added her last known mail address." Ethan said.

"We will pass this on to a friend who lives in Sydney, and he can check it out." Estelle wrote.

"Still some time to go about solving that one then." Esther remarked.

"You should know by now that nothing gets solved in an hour, like depicted on television." Estelle wrote.

"True. One can hope though. Okay, what does the other email say?"

"It says even though I didn't have a last name, that there doesn't seem to be any trace of Kiri." Esther read.

"Maybe Kylie will have the answers to that one."

The following Tuesday afternoon tea had been left set up on a tray. They would give Kylie the choice of sitting in the lounge or out on the deck.

"I can hear a car." Zack commented.

"I think I'll go out and meet her." Esther said as she went out the door.

"Hello Esther." Kylie said, after coming in.

"How did you know? I introduced myself as Diana."

"I was the one that gave you the middle name of Diana. Even though, I'm the one that had the photos taken, the other week, I never saw Felicity in them."

"I can explain that. Mum and Estelle are yet to meet."

"Estelle is it your day to talk or rest?"

"Rest, but how did you know about the accident?" Estelle wrote.

"You'll be surprised at what I know. Esther I think that you had better introduce the others."

"Ethan, Estelle's husband. This is their house, and Zack, my fiancée."

"I know that you probably have lots of questions. What I have to tell you could take some time."

"Would you like to sit on the deck or inside?" Ethan asked.

"Before I decide I have a couple of questions?"

"Ask away." Estelle wrote.

"How did you and Esther meet?"

"At university. We have been friends and business partners for about ten years. We didn't know that we are twins until recently." Estelle wrote.

"Must be frustrating to have to wait for Estelle to answer."

"We are used to it. Probably more frustrating for Estelle." Ethan remarked.

"True, but then I like to think that I'm teaching and learning patience." Estelle wrote.

"Any one good at taking notes on a laptop and listening at the same time?" Kylie asked.

"Actually, I think I will record it and type the notes up later." Ethan remarked.

"I would like to explain without too many interruptions and also take a break at some stage."

There was a chorus of Okays.

"Even though the deck looks inviting, I think indoors is better. First, there's a history of initial birthmarks throughout the family. These are either, on the ankles, behind the knees, on the inside of the elbows, wrists, or either side of the neck and shoulders. The older child, whether male or female, always has the birthmark on their right side. Mine and Kiri are on the inside of our wrists." Showing them her left wrist.

"Kiri married Elijah Woods, their sons, Mitchell and Michael's birthmark is behind their knees, and are the same age as Esther and Estelle. The girls set a record for the first twins to be born close, time wise. They are also third in a line of girls and the only ones so far, to have the birthmarks on the shoulder."

"Our parents Lincoln and Giselle Harding amassed wealth by being stockholders in several big companies. These included oil, power, and telecommunications. Kiri and I were a welcomed change from the four boys, none of which were twins."

"Our parents vetted our boyfriends on the suspicion of them being after our inheritance. My girls Faye and Felicity received a share of that at the age of eighteen, as did Esther. I didn't know, at the time where Estelle was, so I decided to put hers into a trust account. Estelle, I'll inform the trust to release it."

"I think that it is time to take a break. I still have a lot to explain. How about we enjoy this afternoon tea, and I ask some questions. First, where's the bathroom."

"I'll show you." Esther replied.

"That's a lot of information to absorb." Zack commented.

"Maybe you could leave typing it out for the moment, and then perhaps make the connections on the whiteboard later." Ethan commented.

"Makes sense." Estelle wrote.

"Have you and Zack set a date yet? Kylie asked, coming back and sitting down.

"The builders are starting on the house next week. Should take two months. We really haven't discussed a date yet." Zack replied.

Esther was trying to hold back her laughter.

"What's so funny?" Estelle wrote.

"Do share." Zack said, looking puzzled.

"Here I was thinking that we would have a small wedding. I have just realized that our guest list just got a whole lot bigger."

"Does that really matter?"

"I guess not."

"Have you thought where to have the wedding?" Kylie asked.

"Not really."

"Well, now you have at least three options." Kylie remarked.

"We could discuss that later. I did admire your garden."

"I know that Ethan does carpentry. Estelle is a photographer. What about you Zack, Esther?"

"I make and sell jewellery. I designed Esther's ring." Zack said.

"I'm a partner in the photography business with Estelle. I recently qualified as a detective and am now a partner in both businesses."

"Don't you find living and working together, a bit much?" Kylie asked.

"We don't talk business twenty-four seven, or live in each other's pocket." Ethan commented.

"I wasn't suggesting you did. I can see that there's a real deep friendship between all of you, and that's great."

"Can you explain why you changed your mind?" Estelle typed.

"You mean in regard to adding the photos and names of my children."

"Yes."

"I already knew that you two where my granddaughters. I really wanted to get to know you better. I'm not sure whether you were aware that I was watching you while overseas. I was also hoping that some of the people would mention how much you two look a lot like Felicity and Faye. Even though the whole trip was a ruse, it was worth everything I paid."

"Is there anything else, you want to tell us?"

"Yes. While Faye was on holiday in Australia, she met Jacob Balke. He was a New Zealand diplomat that worked at the Australian Embassy. He followed her back here. I tried to warn Faye about his reputation. He had already mentioned that he didn't want children, before he manipulated Faye into marrying him"

"He insisted Faye have a DNA test, when she became pregnant. When it proved that he was the father, he left. However, after the girls' birth, he seemed fixated on Estelle, and even tried to kidnap Estelle on several occasions. I discovered Faye was beaten black and blue when she tried to interfere. I was glad that he went away on a regular basis. Faye decided her only choice was to use one of these occasions to drop Estelle off, at the nunnery."

"When he found out, he went ballistic. She ended up in hospital, with broken ribs, arms, legs broken chin and cheek. She divorced Balke, and was put into protective custody."

"This was where she met and married John Rivers, five years later. They have now been married for over fifteen years. Both became undercover agents, for the FBI. They have the two boys, Adam thirteen, and Cooper eleven. They had been keeping Balke under surveillance, accumulating evidence throughout the years. Last year, Faye and John turned up on my doorstep in disguise. They explained that they were trying to draw Balke out, and the only way to do this was for Faye, to use herself as bait. They set up some recording equipment and then left saying that Faye would turn up in several days time without a disguise. I was to act as I hadn't seen since she left at eighteen. She was right about Balke turning up. He too had been watching the place. The plan was to let him think that he had talked Faye into causing an accident to one of you."

"Balke somehow found where Estelle and Ethan lived and had been watching you both. He took advantage of you dropping one of the cars to the mechanics for its warrant. He went in there and told them that he was a friend of yours and had been asked by you to pick the car up. Both of you were out, when he dropped it back here. It was then he cut the brakes and left."

"He was also the one driving the diplomatic car the night Estelle had the accident. He had put on a women's wig, to try and implement Faye. He tried to ram you several times, as well as running you off the road."

"Faye was the one who hired the bodyguards. There were also several undercover agents at the hospital, including Dee. Faye sat at your bedside, at night, while you were still in the coma."

"They were able to have Balke stripped of his diplomatic ranking. They couldn't extradite him to Australia as he is a New Zealand citizen. Instead, they put him in a prison in Auckland, as far away as possible from here.

With all the evidence accumulated, he will be there for at least twenty years, with no chance of parole."

"Wow, is all I can say." Zack commented.

"We would like you to join us to celebrate our engagement?" Esther asked.

"I'll be away for two weeks." Kylie replied.

"How about we make it for the weekend of the twentieth of this month?" Estelle typed.

"That will work out."

7

"With Kylie being away, it gives us a couple of weeks to organize, and time for you to pick up the ring. Do you think that you can arrange for your Mum to arrive a bit earlier on that day?" Estelle asked a couple of days later.

"Yes. How about an hour or so before?"

"That should be okay. However, we don't say anything about the engagement until everyone else arrives."

"Sneaky. Now, I know we have the same warped sense of humour. But unless we tell the boys about the surprise, they could spoil it."

"True. We had better tell them, then. Explain to your Mum, where we live."

"And that I want her to meet my business partner, and her husband."

"Just don't mention any names."

"Sneaky, but I like."

"It was nice of Gina to help." Esther commented, a couple of days before the dinner, as she came into Estelle's bedroom, and sat in the other lazy boy, next to Estelle.

"Yeah, it was. I did, however, suggest that she makes stuff that she can deliver at lunchtime on the day."

"What's she making?"

"Not sure. I told her what we were planning for the main, and that she could either make the entree, or dessert. Knowing her, she'll do both." Estelle said, smiling.

"Did you tell her to make enough for ten or more?"

"Yep."

"I love this view."

"The view is the same from your room."

"I know, but I don't think I'll ever get sick of it."

"Doesn't your section face the same way?"

"Yes."

"Has the builder seen the new design?"

"Yep."

"Just make sure it makes the most of the view."

"Now, why didn't I think of that?"

"Because I'm the smart one."

"You got the brains, I got the beauty."

"Smarty."

"Am I asking a lot of questions?" Esther asked.

"Not really. It is nice to share the burden." Estelle said.

"Aw gosh. Even though we don't get much chance to go to church, I know that he's listening, and has answered several prayers."

"True."

"How long are you able to talk for now?"

"Up to two and a half hours. I thought that I would save my voice, that day, until dinner."

"Good thinking. Do you think the others will get a shock, when we introduce Felicity?"

"Possibly. It really comes down to whether she confirms she's my birthmother." Estelle said, sighing.

"True, but it is looking more and more likely. Do you think we look alike?"

"Follow me."

"What are you up to?"

"You'll see." Walking into the walk-in wardrobe.

"I do indeed." Esther said, standing next to her, in front of the full length double mirror.

"Okay, we have the same build." Esther said after a couple of minutes.

"Same height." Estelle commented.

"Perhaps the only difference is the hair."

"Not much difference, apart from the length."

"True and your eyes are a darker green." Esther remarked.

"Do you think that we should dress the same that night?" Estelle asked.

"Our taste in clothes is slightly different." Esther stated.

"True."

"Besides, that might be a bit much."

"You could be right."

"I did get some brains after all." Esther said, poking out her tongue.

"Cheeky. You'll keep."

"I'm glad that I'm a keeper, and we found each other."

"I am too. You okay with you and Zack greeting Felicity at the door?"

"You bet."

"Ethan and I'll wait in the lounge."

"Are you looking forward to this?" Esther asked, rubbing her hands together.

"Yes, but I'm also a little nervous."

"That's to be expected."

"I see you picked up the ring."

"What do you think?"

"It's beautiful. It looks custom made."

"It is." Esther said.

"Who made it?"

"Zack." She said proudly.

"Yes, I knew he made jewellery."

"The owner of the shop, where he's been working from the back of, is charging him rent, and then takes a fifteen percent commission on anything that he sells through the shop."

"That doesn't seem fair."

"I checked it out and apparently it is. When we build the house, we are going to add a workshop and a separate shop."

"Good idea. At least making jewellery is not as noisy as carpentry." Estelle smirked.

"I know Ethan is working and I can't hear any noise."

"Only joshing. Can you do me a favour?" Estelle asked.

"Anything."

"Mention that I've a limit for my voice."

"Without saying what happened."

"You got it."

"Sneaky, but I like. I had better get onto the email then."

"See you downstairs then. I'm going to sort through some more of those piles."

"At least we have eliminated three quarters of them."

Estelle decided to send several emails to their contacts, asking for any information with the name Roman Michael Ralph, and added the photo, and pushed send.

8

"Is everything ready to go?" Ethan asked, the day of the dinner.

"Yes. All we have to do is go change."

"Go. I'm sure Zack, and I can manage while you and Esther goes make yourselves even more beautiful."

"Flattery will get you everywhere. Come, Esther."

Estelle and Esther rushed into the lounge, with less than two minutes to go before Felicity arrived.

"Knowing Mum, she'll be either a little bit early or a little bit late." Esther commented, puffing.

"She must have decided to be on time." Estelle said as the doorbell chimed.

"Ready Esther?" Zack asked.

"We had better go and answer the door, then." Esther commented.

Estelle and Ethan stood trying to hear what was going on but failing.

"It will be alright." Ethan said facing her, with his back to the door.

Estelle could hear, but not see, as the three of them came into the lounge/dining room.

"Mum, I would like you to meet Ethan Thorpe." Esther said, as Ethan turned around.

"And behind him is his wife, and my partner."

"Estelle!" Felicity asked "Whoa, I think I need to sit down."

"You alright?" Zack asked.

"I'm fine, really. I just didn't think that I would ever see my other daughter again, and here she is."

"You mean that you tried looking for her, Mum." Esther commented.

"Of course. Did you really think that I wouldn't look for or recognise her? She does look a little bit like Faye."

"So, I have been told." Estelle squeaked.

"I think that you'd better rest your voice for now." Ethan commented.

Estelle gave the thumbs up and picked up her whiteboard, and started writing the questions, she wanted answers to.

"What happened?" Felicity asked, looking concerned.

"She damaged her windpipe in a car accident." Ethan said.

"And she's only allowed to talk for short periods of time, which is now up to two and a half hours." Esther explained.

"Maybe the excitement, of meeting you, has been a little too much for the recovery process." Zack commented.

"You could be right, Zack. Now I see that Estelle has written several questions for you, but I think there are two main ones, what happened in the hospital and where is Faye?"

"I really would like to hug my daughters first, and then show you something, before I explain, and I have some questions of my own."

The men stood back as the three of them hugged.

"This is the only photo I have of Faye and me together." Felicity said, showing them.

"I think Estelle looks more like you Felicity." Zack commented.

"Thank you. Right of this moment, I don't know where Faye is. I have been trying to find her."

"Another name to add to the list, of missing people." Esther commented.

"If you and Faye are twins, why the different surnames."

"Faye and I were very close as we grew up. Our maiden name was Broadmire. I married Doug Ralph in nineteen eighty three. I had Roman by the time Faye married Jacob Balke a year later. She was quite proud that she hadn't had to change her initials."

"Still doesn't explain, the different surnames." Ethan commented.

"I know. The thing is, Doug and I were having problems. Esther, this is not how I wanted you to find out that Doug Ralph isn't your biological Dad. I found I was pregnant after I had a short affair with Jacob. The thing is that Faye and I were pregnant at the same time. Faye insisted that Jacob choose."

"Jacob was very controlling and didn't like being challenged. He said that he had a vasectomy and insisted that we both have DNA tests to confirm that he was the father."

"Both of our marriages split up, as a result. We decided to use the name Broadmire and support each other. However, we both ended up in the hospital at the same time. Knowing that it could get confusing having two F. B's. Faye decided to use the name Fredricks, which was the surname of one of the men that our Mum dated while we were still young."

"Make sense." Zack commented.

"Faye was always boasting that being a mother looked easy. She nearly lost it mentally, when her baby was stillborn. Faye had taken a real liking to Estelle. She was the one that suggested she take Estelle. Even though I wasn't sure, I agreed, because I loved her. However, I did insist that she keep the name Estelle."

"Faye found out very quickly that parenting is not as easy as it looks, especially alone. She would ring nearly every day, asking how she did bathing, or the feeding. I lost contact when she disappeared. I don't even know whether she had any more children." Felicity said with tears in her eyes.

"Are you alright Mum?" Estelle typed, and showed her.

"Yes. Gosh, that's nice for you to feel that you can call me Mum, even if it isn't voiced."

"Did you know that Faye abandoned Estelle?" Ethan asked.

"No, but I wasn't surprised."

"Why not?" Esther asked.

"Even as children, Faye didn't stick to many tasks. By the way Esther, Doug and I got back together when you were about six months old. As you know, we divorced when you were twelve. I was upset that you chose to live with Doug, but I had Roman."

"Even then, Roman and I seemed to spend a lot of time together." Estelle commented.

"You did. Doug and I had shared custody. Every time you ran away, we would find you together."

"How many times did we run away?"

"We lost count."

"Really."

"It's alright; we knew that you were safe with Roman."

"There are a few people arriving shortly. Among them are the people that adopted me." Estelle typed.

"I would like to meet them. They have done a fine job of raising you. Introduce me as your birth mother and call me Felicity."

"That sounds fair." Estelle typed.

"I have a couple of questions before they arrive. How did you both meet?"

"At University, through photography." Esther answered.

"Did you know that you were twin sisters?"

"Not until recently."

"Have we got time for a tour of the photography studio?" Felicity asked.

"That would be fine." Ethan said. "Now, I can see Estelle is looking quizzical, so I'll explain. You know that we are detectives."

"Even I have heard of Thorne Detective Agency."

"Thank you. There's a white board with a lot of information on. This pertains to the case we are working on at the moment, so I covered it."

"We aren't allowed to share any of that info." Esther explained.

"Even I have been sworn to secrecy." Zack commented.

"I guess a tour is out the question then." Felicity said.

"No, it isn't. Follow me everyone." Esther said.

Estelle could see that Ethan had hung several sheets over the whiteboard and then several huge photos on top of that.

"These are good. Who took them?"

"Both of us." Esther replied.

"Why have you got photos of where Faye and I grew up?" Felicity asked as she pointed to some photos on the counter.

"They are not meant to be out." Estelle said softly.

"Too late, now. They are actually for a client, which were meant to be handed over a couple weeks go." Esther said.

"I think we both forgot to give these to her." Estelle typed.

"Is her name Kiri or Kylie?" Felicity asked.

"Who's Kiri?" Zack and Ethan asked together.

"Kylie's twin sister." Esther replied.

"It seems silly to keep information regarding those photos from you." Ethan commented.

"The name of the client is Kylie. What happened? Why didn't I ever meet my grandmother?"

"She cut herself off, from both Faye and I, after you two were born."

"Did she give a reason?" Ethan asked.

"No."

"The other guests will be arriving soon. Enough shop talk for now." Ethan said.

"Gina?" Layla asked, hesitantly, coming in the door within minutes of Paul and Gina.

"Oh my gosh. Layla?" Gina said, hugging Layla.

"How do you know each other?" Ethan asked.

"We had a friend in common." Gina replied.

"That friend nearly tore us apart."

"That's history."

"Do you want to tell us what happened?" Esther asked.

"Like Gina said, its history, and not important. I've thought about you a lot. Wow! What a surprise."

"It seems that it's going to be the day for surprises." Estelle remarked quietly, next to Esther.

"You could be right. You game to see how this plays out?" Esther replied, smiling.

"You bet."

"What are you doing here?" Layla asked.

"Estelle's mine and Pauls adopted daughter. This is Ethan Thorpe, her husband." Gina said making the introductions.

"This is Esther, Estelle's twin sister. They weren't raised together. Zack is Esther's fiancé. This is Felicity, who raised Esther. She's Esther and Estelle's birthmother."

"Wow. Talk about complicated. Well, I'm Zack's birthmother."

"And Ethan's birthmother." Zack said.

"Huh." Layla said.

"I always knew that I had been adopted out at birth. When my parents died, I found the birth certificate, and adoption papers which named you as my birthmother. I then found Zack." Ethan explained.

"I never knew the sex, name, or who adopted the child I had. You and Zack have the same father."

"I think you had better explain." Zack said.

"I married Gavin Johns, and had you Zack. Gavin was a train driver. He was killed accidentally in the shunting yard, when you were eleven months old. It wasn't until after the funeral that I discovered I was already pregnant. I wasn't sure I could handle two children, alone. I therefore decided to put you up for adoption."

"Did you ever remarry?" Gina asked.

"I only met Bryce Woodcock a couple of years ago."

"How come I've never met him?" Zack asked.

"He works two weeks on, two weeks off on an oil rig. He's away at the moment."

"What about a photo?"

"Sure." Layla said, showing them a photo of the two of them together.

"How old is he?" Zack asked.

"He's five years older than me."

"He actually looks younger."

"Everyone says that. However, I've seen his drivers' license." Layla explained.

"Okay." Zack said, sighing.

"You are more technically minded then you portrayed." Ethan commented, after Kylie arrived and laid a very up to date phone on the coffee table.

"Yes, I am."

"Why hasn't Roman contacted me?" Felicity asked.

"He's free to contact you now that the danger has been alleviated. I can see you all looking quizzical, but I assure you, once I have explained you'll see the reason."

"We are only waiting for Richard and Samuel."Gina said.

"Who are they?" Layla asked.

"Our other adopted children."Gina explained. "Both Paul and I discovered early in our marriage that neither of us were able to produce children."

"I never knew that." Estelle typed.

"No big deal. Besides the three of you kept me busy, especially Richard." Gina said, smiling.

"Yeah, he keeps us busy too." Ethan commented.

"Want to do a little payback?" Estelle typed.

"What did you have in mind?" Gina asked.

"Both Esther and I look alike, especially from the back, right?"

"Yes." They all answered together.

"When we dressed tonight we made sure we covered the birthmarks, and had our hair the same. We did, however dress differently."

"I had noticed that." Ethan remarked.

"We have our backs to the door, when he comes in." Estelle typed.

"What about Samuel?"

"I asked him to pick Richard up earlier."

"That was a good idea. Otherwise Richard might not have even turned up." Gina commented.

"My thinking, exactly."

"Samuel already said that he would pick Richard up. I could text him and ask him to play along."

"Without explaining about being a twin?" Gina asked.

"He'll be fine."

"Also ask how far away they are. I'm getting hungry." Zack commented.

Estelle sent the text to Samuel. He replied that they were about five minutes away and put thumbs up at the end.

"I can hear a car." Gina said from the opened door.

"You sure you are alright with this?" Zack asked, standing in front of Esther.

"Zack, quick you stand in front of Estelle, and I'll stand in front of Esther."

"Then he's liable to think that Esther is Estelle."

"My point exactly."

"I like." Zack replied, giving Ethan a high five.

Samuel came in first, followed by Richard.

"Oh good. I'm glad I know some people here. And how's my only sister?" Richard asked, poking Esther, whom he thought was Estelle.

"Estelle is not your only sister, now." Esther said as they both turned to face him.

"What?" Richard spluttered as he looked back and forth at them.

"This is Estelle's twin sister, Esther." Ethan explained. "Even though they have been friends and worked together for several years. They only found out two weeks ago that they are twins."

"Hi Esther, I'm Samuel. Welcome to the family. I think you have managed to confound Richard. I think that this is the first time, that I've seen him speechless."

"Yeah, he's still looking like a goldfish out of water." Paul said.

"You had better make the introductions, Ethan." Gina remarked.

"Got you." Estelle typed, and showed it to Richard.

"What happened? I thought that you were allowed to talk now." Samuel commented.

"She is. Once I've introduced everyone, you might understand that Estelle might be in shock. I thought it best that she does not strain her voice." Ethan explained.

"Before we start, I would like to make a toast." Paul said, after the introductions, and they were sitting down at the table.

"Go ahead."

"To Zack and Esther, a new beginning, Esther and Estelle, found sisters, I, Felicity, Gina Layla, parents who found daughters, and sons, and old friends reunited. And finally, Kylie, mother, and grandmother, and very welcome new friend.

9

Richard, Samuel, and Layla had already left, when Kylie's phone started ringing.

"Excuse me. That will be Faye. She wanted me to leave the phone on. She didn't say why."

All they heard was "Okay, I'll tell them."

"Faye and John don't want anybody going anywhere for now. That will be them." Kylie explained as the doorbell rang.

"Can I answer the door?" Felicity asked.

"Of course." Ethan replied.

It was a few moments before the three of them came into the lounge.

"No need for introductions. I already know you through photos." Faye said.

"A situation has developed. Balke has managed to escape. We believe that he on his way here. We would prefer that everyone is in the one place." John explained.

"Would anyone like to go and get anything from their home?" Faye asked.

"Not really." Zack replied.

"I'm not going anywhere." Paul commented.

"Would you like to explain how he escaped?" Ethan asked.

"He faked appendicitis and went to the hospital, a couple of days ago. The guard that escorted him was about the same build, and height. Basically, he changed places with the guard and walked out. An accomplice helped him with cars, money and a change of clothes. We have been tracking him and know that he has managed to get as far as Wellington." Faye said.

"We also know that Balke has had you all under surveillance through his contacts. We would like permission to check your houses over." John said.

"Isn't that over the top?" Estelle typed.

"We would rather not take any chances." Faye answered.

"We are really sorry that it has come down to this. You must remember that Balke now has a weapon. We have no idea what he could do. We are hoping to corner him before he gets this far. We would rather have you all in the one place, for this reason." John explained.

"Agents are ready to go with you, Felicity, Zack, Paul, Gina and Kylie." Faye said. "Do you have any objection to us checking out this house too?"

"None." Ethan replied.

"We don't know how long this could last. Grab enough for a week."

"The agents won't take long to check your houses so I expect you all back here within an hour."

"Shall I make something for tea?" Estelle wrote, as the others left with the agents.

"That would be a good idea. Want some help?" Esther asked.

"Do you think we have enough beds etc?" Estelle wrote.

"If not we could always hire another motor home." Ethan replied.

"Actually, that's not a bad idea. Faye and I could use that as our base." John commented.

"Okay, I'll organise that." Ethan said, going onto the deck.

"Simon's probably wondering what's going on."

"I will inform him." John commented.

"I guess we will need some food too. Is there anything that you can't eat?" Estelle wrote.

"We are semi vegetarians as well as gluten and dairy free." Faye replied.

"So are we. I guess a shopping spree is on the cards."

"I will go with whoever goes." Faye remarked.

"That would be Estelle and I."

"They have a motor home available, however, there's no one to deliver it." Ethan said.

"Is it far away?" John asked.

"About ten minutes."

"Ring them back and you and I will go and pick it up." John commented.

"Okay."

"I'll get the agents to check the house while everyone is out." John remarked.

Even with five extra people in the house, it still didn't feel crowded, and it was five days long before they got an update.

"Either Balke was speeding on unfamiliar roads, or he fell asleep at the wheel." John said.

"He ended over a bank upside down early this morning. The fire brigade had trouble cutting him out of the car, as his leg was trapped and cut extensively. They tried their best, but he died on the way to hospital." Faye explained.

"So does this mean that it is all over?" Estelle asked quietly.

"Are far as Balke is concerned yes. We are in the process of rounding up all Balke contacts. They will be arrested."

"Do you think he was obsessed?" Felicity asked.

"Possibly. I would like to explain something." Faye commented.

"Personally, I don't think it is necessary."John remarked.

"I know. I was a naive eighteen year old, when I met Balke. I think that I may have had blinkers on to his behaviour. He wanted me to change the prenuptial agreement, to which I wouldn't agree."

"He insisted on the DNA, when Felicity and I became pregnant, as he said that he had, had a vasectomy. He came back when I brought Estelle home. He didn't understand about the sleepless nights etc. He was the one that insisted I ring Felicity. He listened to the phone calls. I worked out that he would disappear for several days at a time. I used this to my advantage when I dropped Estelle off."

"So we are his only offspring." Esther commented.

"Yes. As far as we know." Faye replied.

10

"Wow, this past six months have been busy." Esther said coming into the lounge and plopping down.

"Your wedding preparations alone, would have kept you busy enough without everything else." Estelle remarked.

"True. It has been nice to be able to get together with everyone on a regular basis, especially John and Faye."

"Their boys are delightful. It is nice to see them outside of their job. Have you managed to catch up with Roman?"

"Yes. He suggested that he and Mum walk me down the aisle. I'm still thinking on that."

"You could always just walk down by yourself." Ethan commented.

"I know. How do you feel about what happened?" Esther asked.

"Faye insisted that somebody is with me, even though Balke is dead. At first it felt strange. Then I realised that it was for my protection, and that God was giving me some extra angels in the form of bodyguards. Then I thought that I was pregnant. The test came back negative."

"You realise that it could have been the stress, which caused you to miss a period." Ethan commented.

"I know." Estelle sighed.

"Stop being so hard on yourself." Ethan said.

"I have been giving some thought to names."

"Yeah."

"The thing is anything I chose, like Andrew Nicholas, his initials are going to be A.N.T."

"Does it really matter?"

"No, I guess not. You're probably going to have the same problem, when you marry, with your last name starting with J."

"True, but it is no big deal. And don't forget about the initial birthmark."

"Oh yeah."

"Did you give any thought to my suggestion?"Esther asked.

"To go to the rescue centre and see if we could adopt an animal."

"Yes."

"We gave it a lot of thought and discussion. We thought that we would leave that for the moment. We have quite a bit of work between the two of us." Estelle commented.

"And we thought that we wouldn't be fair to take on something that we perhaps don't have the time and energy for." Ethan added.

"The same could be said about having a child." Esther remarked.

"True. We know that. We decided that we would cross that bridge when we come to it. A lot of people except family, and friends expected us to already have had children, having been married for ten years."

"That's normal. I aren't even married yet, and I have people asking when I plan to start a family."

"Really!"

"Is this your rest day?" Gina asked three days after Esther and Zack's wedding.

"No. It was nice for you three to stay on." Estelle replied.

"Couldn't leave you to do all the cleaning up." Felicity commented.

"It made sense to have Esther dress and leave from here." Gina commented.

"Who thought of the Horse drawn carriage?" Kylie asked.

"That would be me. When Esther told me she wanted to walk from here. I told her, no way." Estelle explained.

"Good on you." Kylie commented.

"I wanted her to feel like a princess for at least one day. Didn't really think that we would get the overflow, guest wise from the wedding." Estelle commented.

"It sort of made sense for the extra to stay here, with you living so close. And they have all departed now. And I'll give you a hand with any extra work, if you want." Gina commented.

"Thanks for that. I'm not really complaining about the extra work. I've just been feeling a little tired lately."

"It's so nice to talk to you without the whiteboard," Kylie commented.

"Hope that it isn't catching. Esther said that she wasn't feeling well either, before they left." Felicity replied.

"Really. How long are they away for?" Estelle asked.

"Three weeks." Felicity replied.

"Do you have much photographic work booked at the moment?" Gina asked.

"Not really. Julia was good enough to space the bookings out."

"That should give you time to get over this bug, or whatever it is."

"And before you ask. I've already taken a pregnancy test."

"There's no harm in a mother hoping, is there?" Felicity said.

"Or an adoptive mother." Gina remarked.

"Or even a grandmother." Kylie added.

"Okay, okay. You guys might have to get your baby fix somewhere else."

"Sorry. We didn't need to put pressure on you."

"I know. I have been thinking it through. I'll wait another month and if no pregnancy, I'll investigate what's going on."

"That makes sense." Felicity remarked.

Estelle was kept busy for the next couple of weeks with bookings of photography clients.

"Did Felicity say why she wanted to see us?" Estelle asked Esther, a week after she and Zack had arrived back.

"Not really. She did mention that she was waiting for me to come back, though."

"What's going on?" Esther asked as Felicity sat down, the next day.

"Where to start?"

"Anywhere you like. You know whatever you say is confidential."

"Yes. I just wish I didn't have to do this in the first place, but it is important, for me to find out the truth, one way or the other."

"Now, you have me intrigued." Esther commented.

"Okay, you already know that I had an affair with Josh Balke. Now just to reiterate. I do regret the affair, but don't regret that I have you two. As you know, Doug had a stroke five years ago. When he went into respite. I packed up most of the house, put it in storage, and downsized. The thing is, I didn't really get a chance to go through all the stuff that went into storage. I have been doing that slowly, over the last year. I found some letters, photos, and other stuff that Doug had kept. There are letters written by Doug to Coral Chamber-Ross, about the same time I had the affair."

"I remember Coral, she worked with Doug. We lived in the same neighbourhood, and the four of us would spend a lot of time together. Coral and I had quite a good relationship, or so I thought. I even used to tease her about her initials. Our friendship seemed to taper off, probably around the same time I had the affair. I know that she was married to Brent and didn't have any children. Even though Coral hadn't told me, I had heard that they couldn't have any."

"I do remember seeing her after Doug and I got back together, and she looked about six months pregnant."

"I would like you to check her out and find out if they did have an affair. I would also like you to find out if there is another sibling for you too, and what happened to Brent and Coral."

"As you know, we collected all the birth certificates, and other information within the two year period that we were born."

"Yes."

"Well, we still have those records. I could go and check whether there's any record for them, right now." Estelle commented.

"Okay." Felicity replied hesitantly.

"Are you ready for this?" Esther asked.

"I hadn't thought past asking you two to investigate."

"Okay." Estelle said coming back. "There's quite a bit here. Shall we have a look together?"

"The first one is a birth certificate for Brenna Pearl Chamber-Ross, born three months after us." Esther said, reading.

"Unfortunately, the next one is a death certificate for the same child at three months old." Estelle commented.

"Is there a cause of death?"

"Yes, S.I.D.S."

"What's that?" Felicity asked.

"Sudden Infant Death Syndrome."

"Does either of those certificates name the father?" Felicity asked.

"No."

"There's another one here, which is the adoption papers for a girl named Melody Rose, a year after that."

"What do you want to do now?" Esther asked.

"Doesn't seem much point in pursuing this much further." Felicity replied.

"Don't you even want to contact Coral?"Esther asked.

"For what purpose? What could I say? Hello, this is the wife of the man I thought you had an affair with, was the child that died his?"

"I see what you mean." Estelle commented.

11

"I think we need to talk." Ethan said after he settled Estelle down on the couch."

"I agree. I have watched you nearly run yourself ragged, these last five days."

"Work is starting to pile up and even though Simon is good, even he is looking a bit worse for wear."

"So what do you think we should do? Can't call Gina, as she and Paul are away for the next five weeks."

"We can't expect them to come home from a holiday that they won."

"No, and Felicity is looking after Esther. Felicity is going to bring her in the wheelchair later, so we can discuss what we do regarding work."

"I have some ideas for you. But that can wait for now. When I found you, you two were laughing so much that it was hard to get any sense out of you. So can you explain what happened?"

"I thought the ambulance staff told you."

"Not really. They just told me that they were taking you two to Dunedin Hospital."

"Okay. As you know the weather has been wet lately, with lots of frost. Esther and I wanted to go and scope out some more possible scene pictures that we can add to the extensive library that we already have. Anyway, I started slipping on a patch of ice, Esther grabbed my arm to try and stop me. We both landed on our bottoms. Both of our phones went flying. I told Esther not to move as I could see by the strange angles of our legs that we might have broken something. We couldn't reach the phones, and of course they landed on the rockery and broke. We called out to you. While we were waiting, Esther suggested that it was a good thing that somebody hadn't filmed what had happened as we could of have ended up on American's Funniest videos. I have always said that some of the videos looked set up, and therefore don't watch. This started us both laughing."

"You gave me a scare."

"I'm sorry."

"Don't do that."

"What?"

"Apologise for something that you had no control over."

"True."

"I also thank God, that you weren't hurt really bad."

"That's true too. I want to ask you how you feel about someone wanting to lease the studio, for a couple of days, on a regular basis."

"I like your suggestion that they bring their own makeup, costume and own catering trucks. And that these trucks don't take up too much room."

"All they are coming to do today is to see if it will work."

"If we do say yes that it is on the condition that they have limited access to the house."

"I thought about that. They could use the toilet and shower by the garage. That way they wouldn't be traipsing through the house. Now, what are your other ideas?"

"I have made some inquiries regarding having a carer living in for the rest of the time. I could carry you downstairs in the morning, after she has helped with showering and dressing."

"That sounds good, but she could find it could be a bit awkward, living in the house."

"What if we hire a motor home again?"

"That could work. But instead of hiring a motor home, why don't we buy one."

"That's a good idea. The other idea I had was what if you two hire one of your classmates from your photography class?"

"They might not have the same visions or eye as they call it that Esther and I do."

"You two could supervise."

"They might find that a little intimidating, with the two of us."

"Maybe. Both of you don't have be there for each session. Work out a roster or something."

"I like. I'll talk to Esther later about that. So, what was the outcome of the inquiries regarding a carer?"

"A lady called Wendy is available, but she would like to meet you first to see if you get along."

"That sounds fair enough. And of course, I have to like her too."

"I'll organise a motor home, regardless of her saying yes or no. I'll go pick it up later. If you two don't like each other, then we try again with someone else."

"I hope that Wendy won't feel that she will be looking after two patients." Estelle commented.

"Why would she think that?"

"When is Wendy due here?"

"Within the next half an hour."

"At the same time that Esther is here. Felicity said that she was going to make the most of the opportunity while Esther is here and do some shopping."

"I see what you mean. With the both of you here, she is liable to think that she has two patients. Especially when I didn't get a chance to explain the whole situation to the agency."

"Ok, I will make it quite clear, when she arrives."

"Phew." Ethan sighed. Do you two have many bookings over the next month or so?"

"About thirty. If we hire one of our classmates like you suggested, then I think we will be alright. Of course, I'll have to explain to the clients. Anyway, Esther and I'll work out how to do that."

"I'll wait until Felicity and Esther arrive, and then I had better get some of this work done."

"Have you thought about hiring some help?"

"Yes. This whole thing might turn out to be quite expensive."

"It's not as if we can't afford it."

"True. But you know me; I still like to be careful. Well, I had better ring someone to order new phones for the both of you as well."

"Okay."

12

"I didn't think that I would be so grateful to see the back of those crutches." Estelle remarked as she and Esther sat relaxing eight weeks later.

"What was it like to see some of the same faces again?"

"Strange, but familiar at the same time."Estelle replied.

"We tried to tell them that it was easier to pick us both up at the same time, and just stagger our Physio sessions."

"I think they finally twigged after a couple of weeks."

"True."

"Now, I can't wait to get out of this moon boot. It is driving me batty, especially being pregnant."

"Congratulations."

"What? You're not going to say you're pregnant too?"

"Why would I do that?" Esther asked.

"Oh, I don't know. We seem to be doing everything else together."

"Just hang on a minute. You are the one that suggested that I join both businesses.

"I know." Estelle said, sighing.

"Are you regretting asking?"

"No, of course not. It's just... No forget it."

"No. You're the one that started this conversation. You might as well finish it."

"It is a bit hard to explain. Growing up, even though I was the only girl, I sometimes felt invisible. Then I met Ethan and you and got to know my identity in Christ. I was rocked by what happened with Balke and his death. And just when my world started being on an even keel again. I feel I'm going to be lost again being a mother."

"Wow. That is probably normal. And just because Felicity and Faye were pregnant at the same time, doesn't mean to say that it is going to happen to us." Esther snapped.

"I didn't say it would. Look, I'm sorry. Can we put this conversation down to pregnancy hormones?"

"I guess we could. Are you going to find out whether you're having twins or not?"

"I think that might be wise."

"True. Do you think some time apart would help?" Esther asked, nearly in tears.

"No, of course not. Come here." Estelle said, hugging Esther. "Look, I'm sorry I upset you. But I think I'm just questioning my ability to be a mother."

"I don't think that you would be the first one to do that."

"True. And I'm sure God will give me the ability to cope."

"That's better. And of course, you'll have plenty of help whether you have one child or two."

"I keep forgetting that."

"I guess that is part of growing up in a small family."

"You grew up in a small family too." Estelle replied.

"Yes, I did. But I also felt secure. Growing up knowing that you were adopted probably changed your perception of that security."

"I never thought of it that way. Thank you,"

"For what?"

"Being the wiser one."

"What else are older sisters for? Now we probably need to discuss a few things. Like, what to do about the detective business?"

"Yes, it does seem to have slowed right down." Estelle remarked.

"It is probably a good thing at the moment."

"True. We do have some cases that are now closed and need filing, but, that is about it."

"And Pauline is coping with the clients from the photography business."

"Do we need to advertise?" Esther asked.

"We never had to before."

"True."

"You know what I feel like doing?"

"What?"Esther asked.

"Hopping in the spa."

"That sounds like a good idea. Got a spare swimsuit?"

"Yes. And the spa will hopefully stop the itch."

"Could do. But the itchiness could also mean that the leg is getting better."

"True. You go find that swimsuit. There should be one in the changing room for the swimming pool. I'm going to get a drink of orange on my way through."

Right. Drink, tick. Changed into a swimsuit, tick. Well, one, which fits. Now, to get this moonboot off. Better sit down here, feeling rather woozy.

"Estelle! Wake up! Come on hon." Ethan pleaded.

"Come on Estelle. I rang the ambulance. They should be here soon." Esther said.

Once again, there was a slight fogginess and an uncertainty of what had happened. She could hear familiar voices urging her to wake up. She tried to shake her head to try and clear it, with little success.

"Try and keep still." Ethan urged. "Esther found you on the floor, in the spa. We think that it is wise you don't move until the paramedics have checked you out. As we are not sure where the blood on the floor is coming from."

"What about the baby?" Estelle asked, putting her hand on her stomach.

"What did you say? We saw your mouth move, but nothing came

out. Esther's gone to get the whiteboard. It could just be shock. Ah, I hear the ambulance."

The next half an hour seemed to go excruciatingly slow with people poking, prodding, and asking questions in all directions, which she couldn't really answer.

"It has been decided to put you in hospital for observations. They don't think that there is any damage to the baby but thought it would be wise to do an ultrasound, just to check. However, you did manage to reopen your wound on the leg and that is where all the blood is coming from. Esther has packed a bag. I'll follow you in my car." Ethan explained.

"What do you think?" Ethan asked, several hours later after all the tests and ultrasound.

"Not quite sure what to think. I'm still taking it all in."

"At least you got your voice back."

"True. However, it is a little annoying, every time something happens, that it seems to affect my voice."

"Yeah, I was thinking about that too. Didn't they say after the accident that shock or trauma can affect it?" Ethan commented.

"Yes. Not sure, that I'm ready for this, yet." Estelle said, patting her stomach.

"You knew that there was a possibility of having a multiple birth, right?"

"Of course. I was prepared for twins, but not for the fact that it is triplets, and that I'm five months, instead of three, was the shocker. We only have four months to prepare."

"What do you think we can decide now?"

"Work commitments, where they sleep, and names."

"Ok. My work is slowing down a little, and I have regular customers that have ongoing orders." Ethan said.

"Good. What about Simon?"

"Looks like he wants to set up on his own."

"That makes sense. Did you notice that he and one of the models of the shoots seemed to have hit it off?"

"He said that her name is Chantal. He has asked her to marry him. Anyway, it looks like they will move to Taupo, his hometown. Chantal comes from Rotorua."

"Do you think that you'll be able to do all the work on your own?"

"Don't have to. Have a list of names, who want to be the next apprentice." Ethan commented, laughing.

"Is that because of the live on site accommodation?"

"Possibly. But there's something that I would like to do for Simon and Chantal. I would like to buy them a bigger motor home as a present. Simon plans to build on some land up there but won't have anywhere to live while doing the build."

"I don't have any problem with that." Estelle commented.

"Didn't think you would. They get married next month before leaving to go up north, and want to take their time driving up, as part of their honeymoon."

"What a good idea. Looks like I might not be able to attend as the doctors have insisted on bed rest while here, and limited work when I go home."

"Good thing too. Don't worry, Esther will take plenty of photos. What about the people leasing the studio?"

"It is down to once a month. So, I think that it will alright. Esther and Pauline are handling the photography clients. Esther is also representing me at the court cases. All she has to do is give them my notes. She won't have to talk or anything in court."

"Good. We wouldn't want her to be doing anything illegal. Esther did say that she had taken photos of all the jewellery that Zack makes, and posted the photos on a web page, she set up, and wants to make up a booklet to distribute. Esther said that they could have enough orders from the website to keep him busy for the next two years. He is training someone too. They sell quite a bit from their shop."

"Okay, work is sorted. And we can always be flexible. What about where they sleep."

"I was thinking of having them in our room for the first six months or so." Estelle said.

"They could be in one of the other rooms right from the start, if we have baby monitors."

"Are you okay with that?" Estelle asked.

"Yeah, if you are."

"Okay, then we set up the first room, closest to us, as the nursery, to start with and set up two others for when they get bigger."

"So, a shopping spree is on the cards. Gina and Esther might have to help with that one, seeing how you'll be here."

"We don't have to change much in the other rooms at the moment."

"True. But I suggest we at least get the furniture needed. And don't forget that you can call on all the help you want."

"True. It is just the logistics of three of everything that sort of blows my mind."

"I'm sure we'll cope."

"Why didn't you want to know what sex the babies are?" Ethan asked.

"I thought that it might be nice to wait and see. Now I'm not sure what the surprise of having them will do to my voice."

"We can always ask for the results now."

"True. Well, we know that it is three. It could be three boys or three girls."

"Or two of one sex and one of the other." Ethan commented.

"Hadn't thought of that."

"I have just texted the doctor who did the ultrasound to ask for the results."

"So, while we are waiting. What names do you like?"

"How about you write the names down and I'll do the same and we compare."

"Sounds good."

"Ready to see the results and compare names?" Ethan asked ten minutes later."

"Ready."

"Ta dah." Ethan said as he opened the envelope and held it so they could both see.

"Two boys and a girl."

"Now for names. If we both have the same names on our separate lists, then I think that it could be a good indication of the first name." Ethan commented.

"Whoops, don't forget they will have initial birthmarks somewhere on their bodies." Estelle commented.

"Nearly forgot about that. Then we are going to have to hope that it is a K, as we both have Kramer, Konrad and Kezia."

"They're all nice. What about middle names?" Estelle asked.

"How about Kramer Jared, Konrad Xavier, Kezia Heather."

"That sounds really nice."

"We had better pick some other names, just to be on the safe side."

"I see we both have names starting with D, J, and M. Declan, Devyn, and Dharma. "Estelle commented.

"We could leave the middle names the same for those three. Let's add Jake Xavier, Joel Konrad, and Julia Kezia."

"How about Michael Xavier, Mitchell Konrad, and Michelle Catherine?"

"That sounds okay. Now to tell the others, the latest news, about our three bundles of joy."

"They'll get a shock." Estelle giggled.

"True. Let's keep their names to ourselves for now."

"I like. Shall we tell them that it is two boys and a girl?"

"Yeah, why not."

"Hope you don't go a little stir crazy, being confined to resting, when you come home?"

"I have a few projects up my sleeve."

"Like what?"

"Fixing some of my clothes, a lot of reading, and resting."

"Don't think you have much choice in the resting."

"True. I'll get Esther to get me some Christian based library books. We seem to have the same tastes, so I'm sure, what she picks will be fine."

"Good idea." Ethan commented.

"Could you buy me some loose kaftans?"

"Do you think that you can trust me on the colour choices?"

"You could always ask Gina to go with you, she knows what I like. I only want six in a size 12."

"The shopping spree will have to be later on today,"

"Okay. When are the others coming?"

"Shortly. I sent a mass text to them telling them to come at two o'clock, okay?"

"Good, then I get to have lunch. I could get used of this, being waited on." Estelle said, rubbing her hands together as nurse an aide brought in a tray.

"There are two meals here." Ethan commented.

"My name is Heidi, and I've been told to deliver two on the doctor's insistence."

"That isn't normal hospital policy?" Estelle commented.

"No, it's not. Seeing how your doctor is the head of staff, he's allowed to bend the rules occasionally."

"How will they know if I'm going to be here for every meal?" Ethan asked.

"Don't know. All I've been told to do is deliver two. If your wife is the only one here, then the other will be put in the staff fridge."

"Okay, thanks" Ethan said as she left. "I see that she's put two order menus on here for tomorrow."

"So, I guess I'm not the only that is going to get spoilt." Estelle commented.

"Looks good."

"What are you two up to?" Esther asked, coming into the room, about an hour later.

"Just resting. Oh man you gave me a fright." Ethan said. "Where's everyone else?"

"Outside, checking whether they can all come in at once. The hospital policy says only two visitors at a time."

"Apparently, we are all allowed, anytime while you are here and no limit to the number either." Felicity said as she came in followed by Paul, Gina, Zack, John and Kylie.

"Faye couldn't be here," John commented.

"Seems that we are bending a few of those hospital policies." Estelle commented.

"Now, I called you all here, to share some good news." Ethan said as he sat on the edge of the bed and took hold of Estelle's hand. "Yes, I know, you know that we are having a baby, but what you don't know is how many. It's good that you are all sitting down. We have found out that we are having two boys and a girl."

"What?" Paul exclaimed.

"Triplets. That will certainly be a first in the family." Kylie said.

"Faye's not going to believe this," John remarked.

"Felicity?" Estelle asked. "Did you have several lots of names picked out for Esther and myself?"

"Sort of. We somehow felt that it was alright just to have, say five letters of the alphabet picked out. Then we had to wait and see."

"I can't wait to meet these three." Gina commented.

"I'll contact the Multiple Birth Club, for you. They have all sorts of information and contacts that will be useful." Kylie remarked.

"Good thinking." Felicity said.

"I was just thinking that there seems to be a pattern to the initials birthmark." Kylie said.

“What do you mean?” Gina asked.

“We started with a K, then F, then E. If I’m right. Your three could have D.” Kylie explained.

“Guess we will have to wait and see.” Ethan replied.

13

During the next week, while still in hospital, Ethan and Estelle managed to choose all the stuff required. This was done by looking at photos on a web site on her laptop. Estelle was pleased that the Doctor had said that she was going to be released the following day, as she was starting to go a little bit stir crazy.

"The Doctor said limited exercise, for the rest of the pregnancy." Esther commented, as she and Ethan helped pack her stuff.

"Am I allowed to at least climb the stairs?" Estelle asked.

"No other option but to climb the stairs. We did think that it would be nice if you had some company. How would you feel about that?"

"Sounds good, as long as no one minds if I don't talk much or go to sleep on them."

"They have sort of made up a roster. And towards the seventh month there's going to be a care giver living in the mobile home."

"The doctor did say that they might be born early."

"Some women did a spring clean throughout the house the other day." Ethan commented.

"How did Mrs Peterson feel about that?"

"She was the one that suggested it. She also said that she would like to retire. She has asked if her daughter Karla can take over from her as she's going to have a hip replacement operation within the next month."

"That's okay with me. I'm looking forward to seeing all the stuff we ordered, delivered."

"It arrived yesterday. I thought that I would wait for you to be home before we set it all up."

"Thanks for that."

"Several people from the Multiple Birth Club have rung re having family photos done. I thought that it might be nice to offer them some sort of discount." Esther said a couple of days after Estelle had come home.

"What a good idea. You know that as a partner that you don't have to run any ideas pass me?"

"Of course, I just thought that it would be courteous to let you know. We already have about ten families booked."

"Are you part of the roster?"

"I have tried to coincide it with the days that have Multiple Birth Club bookings. You or Pauline will be doing the other bookings."

"Do we have a lot of bookings?"

"About six a day. I have tried to make sure the regular bookings are spaced to three in the morning and three in the afternoon. As for the Multiple Club, I book them for Tuesday or Thursday, and do the same there. I have tried not to book any sessions on the weekends."

"I wonder if the doctor would consider taking photos as exercise." Estelle commented.

"Not sure." Esther giggled. "You can always do the session sitting down, and either Pauline or I'll do the set up."

"That sounds good."

Estelle was waiting for a few people to turn up to the meeting that she had called, after three weeks at home.

"At the moment it feels like a train station here. Now, I know that you are all concerned about me, but being watched all the time is a bit overwhelming. I'm quite capable of texting or ringing someone if I have a problem. I don't want any of you to put your lives on hold to monitor me." Estelle said.

"I'm sorry we made you feel that way." Paul said.

"I'm here almost every day to do with the photography business, so how do we change that?" Esther commented.

"We are sorry." Gina, Paul, Zack, and Felicity said together.

"How about cutting back on the photography to twice a week? Felicity asked.

"That might work." Esther replied. "I might have to anyway, as it has just been confirmed that I'm pregnant."

"Congratulations." Estelle remarked.

"The other option is to let Pauline do all the work and either of you check in with her, on the days you decide to work." Felicity said.

"True." Estelle and Esther replied together.

Esther and Estelle managed to get their scans and checkups to coincide. It was at Esther's second scan that she was told that she was having twin boys. The thing was that one of them was a lot smaller than the other and the doctors were concerned.

"How do you feel about having twin boys?" Estelle asked, once they were home.

"You know what, I'm not sure I can handle twins." Esther replied.

"The logistics of three is still a little overwhelming."

"Yeah. Sorry I didn't think."

"Everyone says that we can call on them etc. But I wonder how long the novelty will last."

"And the reality of looking after two or even three at one time sets in."

"Sounds like pregnancy hormones have set in and you two are having a down day." Ethan remarked as he came into the lounge.

"Do you have to sneak around like that? Estelle asked,

"I wasn't sneaking around as you call it. You two were so engrossed that I doubt if a herd of elephants going through here would have made any difference."

"Ok. We agree not to try to allow the pregnancy hormones to get us down." Estelle said.

"Speak for yourself." Esther commented. "I agree in principal, on the one condition that we tell each other if we are feeling down and put some music on."

"Those days may not coincide." Ethan remarked.

"True. But whether they do or not, there will be more music." Estelle stated.

Estelle was hospitalised in her eight month and had only been there a couple of weeks when Esther was rushed in with suspected eclampsia. The hospital staff decided that the girls could be in a double room.

Together, the doctors and Estelle agreed on a date of August fifteenth two thousand and seventeen, which was now only a day away, to deliver the children by caesarean birth.

"Have you thought of names yet?" Estelle asked, sitting on the bed puffing, after their daily two laps of the wards.

"How about you tell me the names you have, and I'll tell you mine." Esther replied, puffing as well.

"Well, I guess you will know soon enough."

"True. I have gotten used to the idea of twins, now."

"Now, we get lost in the identity of being a mother."

"Nothing wrong with that."

"True. Sometimes, someone who knows Gina says 'Oh, you're Paul and Gina's daughter."

"Still nothing wrong with that."

Once again, Estelle could hear people calling her to wake up.

"Don't you want to meet our little family?" Ethan asked.

"We know that you're groggy. That is a result of the anaesthetic the doctor gave you." Esther commented.

Estelle wanted to see the babies, but also wanted to go back to sleep. Sleep won over for the next couple of hours. Finally, she felt more awake when the nurse was about to hand her one of the children.

"We haven't put name tags on them yet as Ethan said he would be here soon. Would you like to hold one and see the other two?" Connie the nurse asked.

"Can I?" Estelle squeaked.

"We thought that might happen, so I have brought the white board in."

"Can I sit up and you lay the three of them on the bed and put pillows, so they don't fall off?" Estelle wrote.

"Of course."

"So how do I breast feed all three?" Estelle asked quietly.

"That's easy." Ethan said, walking in. "Rotate them. You're not going to be able to feed two at once, anyway."

"True." Estelle replied.

"The other thing is that all the mums from the Multiple Birth club have offered to donate breast milk and have it delivered." Connie said.

"Don't worry. They have said that it will be delivered both here and to our house." Ethan added.

"Now, I'm not saying that it will be easy, especially with three. Getting into a routine will help. "Want a photo?" Connie asked.

"Of course."

"I'll leave you two with your little family so you can decide their names." Connie said after the photos.

"Did you know that they haven't got any birthmarks?" Ethan asked.

"Really. So that means that we don't have to give them names with the same initial." Estelle wrote.

"Unless we really want to."

"I don't think we could be that mean." Estelle wrote and laughed quietly.

"So, do you think we can decide on names?"

"I don't know. I like one name on each list." Estelle wrote.

"Okay. How about we each write the names down that we like and then compare?"

"That could work."

"Okay. Let's compare." Ethan said ten minutes later. "Our girl will be easy, Kezia Michelle." Ethan commented, after looking at Estelle's list written on the white board.

"So, which one looks like a Xavier Joel?" Estelle wrote. "And which one will be Devyn Kramer?"

"We could go Enny Menny Minny Mo." Ethan suggested.

"I somehow don't think they would appreciate that." Estelle wrote, and added a frowny face.

"Yeah, you're probably right. Wouldn't go down well, when we tell them."

"Okay, executive decision here. From the left Xavier Joel and Devyn Kramer on the right." Estelle wrote.

"You know, of course, that it wouldn't have made any difference if they had been born with the birthmarks." Ethan commented.

"True. They will soon develop their own personalities, and let's try and treat them as individuals."

"They are probably always going to be known as the triplets or even the Thorne triplets." Ethan commented.

"Yeah, I guess. We can still treat them as individuals."

"Okay, let's put their name bands on."

14

The children had been home six weeks and had settled into a routine quite easily.

Esther now came over two days a week, and brought her twins, with her. The doctors had been wrong about it being two boys, and they didn't have any birthmarks either. Esther had a boy first and named him Keith Jordan and three hours later a girl Paige Melody, made an appearance, which set a record.

"I don't know how you do it?" Esther commented after she had placed the twins in the spare cot upstairs and put the double pushchair into the empty space of the photography studio.

"Do what?"

"Manage with three. What I have to bring when I come here, is a little bit mind blowing."

"You were a Kindergarten teacher." Estelle commented.

"Your point being?"

"That you would have learnt how to manage more than one child at a time."

"Yes, that is true. However, the children in kindergarten are at least three, and there are other helpers. It is somehow different when it is your children, and they are smaller."

"You have a home help too."

"True. I'm trying not to get too used to her being around."

"Yeah. I know what you mean. Mine leaves in a couple of days." Estelle sighed loudly.

"Okay, do we need to put some music on?"

"Not right now. I would just like to sit and listen to the silence of knowing all five of them are asleep."

"I think we need to talk." Esther said a couple of minutes later.

"That sounds serious."

"Not really. But we do need to discuss both businesses."

"Well, the detective agency has taken a downturn for the moment." Estelle said.

"And any cases we have are just about wrapped up."

"We are nearly all caught up with all the Multiple birth Club bookings." Estelle said.

"You know, of course, that neither of you have to work." Ethan said coming through from the workshop.

"There you go, sneaking around again." Estelle said.

"Guilty as charged. I'm playing hooky from work. Kylie rang, and said she wanted to talk to all of us. I know what it is about, but I think I will let her explain. She said that she had already spoken to Zack, and he's on his way too. I peeked in on all five children."

"You're not going to tell us what Kylie wants to talk about." Estelle commented.

"You'll both have to be patient." Zack said coming in. "Ethan and I are standing together on this one."

"Looks like they are serious." Esther commented.

"I think they both need to work on their serious looks." Estelle giggled, seeing Ethan pulling faces.

"Yeah. They are both goofs." Esther said.

"But they're our lovable goofs." Estelle said.

"You two are more like Laurel and Hardy than superman types." Esther remarked.

"You two will keep as I just heard a car pull up." Ethan replied.

"Now, I know Ethan and Zack know what this is about, but they don't know all of it. I want all of you to hear me out. Some of the questions that you might have will be hopefully solved by the time I've finished. First, I think that a cuppa is in order, and while someone is doing that, there are some bags in my boot, that need to be brought in. And while that is being done we will just sit and relax." Kylie commented as she came in.

Estelle looked at the two big luggage cases that Zack had brought in, several minutes later, as they sat with a coffee pot on the table and helped themselves.

"No. I'm not moving in." Kylie commented. "Apart from some toys on the top for all five of my great grandchildren, most of it is everything I could find, to do with Kiri."

"So, you still want us to find her? Ethan asked.

"Of course." Kylie replied.

"Do you want to tell us why you lost contact with her?" Esther asked.

"Some other time, perhaps. Now, what I really came here to talk about. First, I don't see enough of my great grandchildren or any of you. I know that is not all your fault. My schedule has been a little bit up and down lately, but that is going to change. Second, I'm a little disappointed that none of you felt that you could call on me either babysitting or financially wise."

"You see, you lot are not the only detectives in the family. I have done a little discreet digging into both of your bank records. How did I do that, I hear you ask? I used my name and pulled a in a few favours here and there. I know that you will probably say that you don't need my help financially but look upon it as an investment into both yours and my great grandchildren's lives. Before I explain, could we take a break, as I think I hear a couple of those great grandchildren?"

Estelle found it interesting watching as the others chose which baby they would feed, bathe, change and have some one on one time with. It was two hours later by the time all five babies were settled again.

"That was almost like a military operation." Kylie commented as they sat in the living room.

"It often becomes that when we have all five here at once." Esther replied.

"Now I know that some of what I have in mind might help."

"Okay, I think I have been very, very patient." Estelle commented.

"First the financial help. Like I said, look upon this as an investment. I have deposited a hundred thousand dollars into both of your accounts. I have also set fifty thousand dollars for each of the children into six term investments, which will keep turning over until the children are eighteen. Half of the interest from those investments will go automatically back into your main accounts. The other half will turn over with the investments. Yes, I know that there are only five children, but I like to give to the girls equally. I will also set up investment accounts for any future children."

"I don't have a problem with that." Estelle said, squeakily.

"I'm gobsmacked." Esther said.

"So even surprises can affect your voice." Ethan commented.

"Not sure how I'm going to cope with the children if my voice gives out all the time." Estelle wrote.

"You'll think of something." Zack replied.

"I could always use a whistle like Captain Von Trapp did in the 'Sound of Music." Estelle wrote.

"You couldn't or wouldn't be that cruel." Ethan remarked.

"You know me too well." Estelle wrote.

"Good thing, as you're stuck with me."

"You're the only I want to be stuck with." Estelle wrote and put hearts all over the whiteboard.

"Ah." Ethan commented giving her a shoulder hug.

"Okay, you two, enough of that for now." Kylie said. "Now, I've set up a spa day, for Estelle and Esther, once a month."

"It'll be nice if we could do it together." Esther commented.

"Yes, it would, what about the children?" Estelle wrote.

"I'm sure that we could work something out, between me, the grandparents, or uncles." Kylie said.

"True."

"The first spa day is set for tomorrow."

"Tomorrow!" Exclaimed Esther. "Oh well, it will be nice to relax."

"What time tomorrow?" Estelle wrote.

"Ten. Now, I have organised Gina, Paul, and myself to be here at eight thirty in the morning. Be warned that you will be pampered and from what I have been told, you won't be home until after seven. Now, Esther, Layla and Felicity will be at your place about the same time and will help you bring the twins here. We thought that it would be easier to have all five babies in one place. You two will then be picked up around nine thirty."

"I would also like to shout the four of you a weekend away. Now, I knew you wouldn't want to go too far, so the Mandalay is just outside of Dunedin. I set the first weekend away for next weekend. No arguments, please. They are expecting you on either late Thursday night or Friday morning. I would like you lot to use this every month, if possible."

"We can't say no to that." Zack remarked.

"I wouldn't want to say no to that." Ethan replied.

"Last, but not least. How long before the children wake." Kylie asked.

"Probably an hour or more." Estelle replied.

"That will give us some time to talk about where your businesses are and where to from here."

"I was just saying to Esther before, that we are nearly all caught in the photography business." Estelle said.

"And you are our one and only client, on the detective side." Esther remarked.

"How's the workshop doing Ethan?" Kylie asked.

"I have orders backed up for the next five months. Among them are special orders, which will bring in quite a bit of revenue."Ethan said. "I have one apprentice, and he's doing very nicely."

"And what about your jewellery Zack?"

"I have orders backed up, for the next two years, thanks to the brochure and the online site. Most of those will be filled, thanks to my three apprentices, within the next six months. I have explained all this to the clients, and they are happy with that."

"Don't forget about the special orders." Esther piped up.

"I wouldn't forget them. These are the ones that have allowed me to employ the apprentices. I am working on the special orders." Zack said.

"How many special orders do you have?" Kylie asked.

"Ten, all together. Currently I'm working on three. Don't worry, I know, which is which."

"Phew." Estelle wrote.

"I would also like to suggest that you run the photography business as a hobby, instead of as a business."

"That could work." Estelle remarked.

"Let's look at it in another six months time, and then see." Esther suggested.

"That's probably a good idea." Estelle replied.

"Now, I suggest that you all get an early night, if possible." Kylie said.

<h1 style="text-align:center">15</h1>

"Estelle, hon. Wake up, you were calling out." Ethan said, shaking her, a couple of days after their fourth weekend away.

"How long have I been asleep?" She asked, as she rubbed her eyes with the dream of Jacob catching her still fresh in her mind.

"Don't know. I came in to get a drink when I heard you calling out. Want to tell me what you were dreaming about?"

"Jacob catching me."

"You know that's not possible."

"Yes, but it doesn't stop my mind."

"It was only a dream."

"Tell me something. How would you feel if you put the lives of your family and yourself in the line of danger?"

"Probably the same as you. Come here." Ethan said as he drew her into his arms. "I think that you need to talk to someone about these thoughts."

"I agree, but I already feel guilty enough about taking time away from the children with the spa days and the weekends away."

"Don't you think you deserve that time?"

"Sort of."

"Nothing has happened, right."

"True."

"Don't you think that I think about them, when we are not here?"

"You don't show it." Estelle said with tears starting to roll down her cheeks.

"Yes, I know I portray the strong Tarzan type."

"Sort of."

"I'm sorry I gave you that impression. I'm more like a Lion wanting to protect. Just remember I'm new to being a parent too."

"It would help if you showed it more."

"I'm working on it. I could say the same that you shouldn't worry too much."

"Yeah, I'm a worry wart."

"I didn't quite mean it that way." Ethan replied.

"Okay. Here's something to mull over. I want to wait before having any more children." Estelle said.

"So, you are not ruling out having more."

"Of course not."

"The doctor's said one of the possible reasons for you having a multiple birth was you being on the pill."

"Yes, I remember that. I would like to wait until they're three before even thinking about getting pregnant again."

"Sounds fair enough." Ethan remarked, before starting to laugh.

"What tickled your fancy?"

"The irony of that."

"Huh."

"Waiting three years and they will be three. No, I can see you don't get it, so it must be my sense of humour." Ethan said.

"Probably. This is nice."

"You mean having time to ourselves."Ethan answered.

"Yes."

"Do you know if Esther has the same thoughts about Jacob?"

"I haven't even asked her?" Estelle answered.

"Don't you think you should, and also talk to a professional?"

"I'll ask Esther, but I don't know any professional counsellors who are Christians."

"Neither do I. May be either Gina or Kylie does."

"I didn't really want to involve either of them in this, but I might have to."

"You're going have to trust someone."

"Yeah, you're right." Estelle sighed.

"Actually, it might be better if you contact Kylie." Ethan remarked.

"That could be a point. I could tell Gina, but she could go all mama bear. Esther's coming tomorrow as well, so she might even know someone in her circle of contacts."

"True. You know, of course, that we are both going to have to start trusting other people with our children."

"We already do."

"They are members of the family. I meant people outside the family. What about when they go to kindergarten, etc."

"They aren't even going to kindergarten, and you have got them going to university."

"Don't exaggerate." Ethan said.

"I guess we need to both take a breath and calm down." Estelle remarked exasperatedly. "Do you want some music on?"

"No, I like the sound of silence, knowing that they are safe. Gina mentioned that they took all five of them for a walk the other day."

"What?"

"Now before you go mama bear on me. She said that even though it took a little organising, they took them down to the park."

"I'm not going all mama bear, I'm just gobsmacked. We might have to start doing that."

"You mean taking them to the park."

"Yes, but we could do with some help."

"Maybe for the first couple of times. But once we get the hang of it. I think we will be okay."

"Okay, let's see what happens."

"Like I said we have to trust people. The house hasn't fallen down. The children haven't called out and said don't leave us Mummy or Daddy."

"Oh, you goof they are only four months old."

"True."

"You may have noticed that area there. I have started to bring them down here."

"Who gives you a hand with that?"

"No one. It could trickier as they get bigger."

"You could be right about that."

"You know that with these three and the prospect of having more children we have lost our guest bedroom." Estelle remarked.

"We do have the motor home."

"True."

"The other pro about having no room at the inn, so to speak is that Richard has to actually call beforehand, to see if the motor home is available."

"Yeah," Estelle smirked. "But he also loves spending time with all of them. And the motor home does become vacant on a permanent basis when the current home help leaves."

"Then we will be back to the normal routine of Karla coming in."

"I don't think anything will be normal in this house again."Estelle said, laughing.

"True. But it is our normal and I for one like it."

"Me too, I think. I think I can hear them, stirring, want to help me bring them down here for awhile?"

"I like that idea. And then I can spend some time with all four of you."

"Don't you have any work?"

"Nothing that can't wait until later or even tomorrow. I've also been thinking about adding a double storey extension." Ethan commented.

"Do we need it?" Estelle asked.

"We do if we are planning on having more children, unless you want them to live in the motor home."

"Very funny. How about if you start building in a year or so."

"That sounds like a good idea. I'm looking forward to having a bit of time with you later."

"I like your thinking Mr Thorne."

"After you Mrs Thorne before they start screaming the place down."

16

"**D**o you think my two can join your three down there, on the floor?" Esther asked, coming into the lounge the next day.

"Don't see why not, there's heaps of room." Estelle replied.

"At least we don't have to worry about them being woken up by any noise coming from the workshop."

"Nope. We also don't have to worry about keeping our voices down either. I want to ask you a few questions, once you have finished, so I'll put the jug on." Estelle remarked.

"Okay."

"What do you want to ask your wise and older sister, and friend?" Esther asked, plopping herself on the couch and putting her feet up.

"Do you ever have thoughts or dreams about Jacob?"

"No, why have you?"

"Yes. Several times, and I fell asleep yesterday and dreamt that he caught me."

"How many times have you had these dreams?"

"Yesterday was the first time that I dreamt that he caught me. I've had the dreams off and on since we were all held captive here."

"We weren't held captive as you put it."

"How would you put it, then?"

"Faye wanted us to be safe and in one place."

"I know that, but some of my thought patterns are a little skewed."

"I think I understand that, and what do you mean about having the dreams off and on."

"The dreams stopped when I was pregnant and have now come back."

"Does Ethan know this?"

"Some of it."

"Which part does he know?"

"About yesterdays' dream. He suggested I need to talk to a counsellor."

"He's right about that."

"That's part of my problem. I don't know any Christian counsellors."

"Neither do I."

"Ethan suggested that I contact Kylie."

"What a good idea. Would you like me to contact her and explain?"

"Would you mind?"

"Of course not. Would you like me to come with you?"

"If it is possible." Estelle replied.

"I'll support you in any way I can."

"I feel like a coward?"

"What do you mean? It takes strength to admit that you have a problem and decide to do something about it."

"I don't feel strong."

"How about I give Kylie a ring now, and then we can go from there."

"Okay."

Estelle could only hear some of the one sided conversation as Esther had gone into the hallway to talk to Kylie.

"Right, the Lord has worked rather quickly in answering this particular prayer. At first, she said that she didn't know anyone, and then suddenly she remembered a friend of hers, who is a counsellor. She put me on hold while she rang her and set up an appointment for this Wednesday at ten am."

"That's only a couple of days away." Estelle remarked.

"Do you have a problem with that?"

"No, not really."

"Don't you dare wimp out by using the children as an excuse? The children will be here anyway."

"I'm not going to wimp out. It just means that we get an extra-long weekend."

"You're the one that suggested moving the spa day to the day before the weekend away."

"It made sense." Estelle said, shrugging her shoulders.

"Hope I haven't overstepped, but I rang Gina and told her about the appointment."

"What did she say?"

"She seemed pleased about getting an extra day."

"No, I meant about me going to see a counsellor."

"She didn't seem surprised. I also said depending on the length of the appointment that we might do some shopping, for us."

"That sounds a good idea. The children have enough clothes to last until next century."

"That's a wee bit of an exaggeration, but I know what you mean."

"I do agree that I need some clothes."

"I think you might be right about putting the photography business on hold until the children get older." Esther remarked a couple of minutes later.

"What about Julie, and Pauline. They have been very helpful."

"How about we give them money? After all, we will need their help when we restart."

"They might not be available." Estelle said.

"True. Let's cross that bridge when the time comes."

"How much were you thinking?" Estelle asked.

"At least five grand. I know for a fact that Pauline could use that."

"Let's make it ten each. The photography business will cover that."

"True. Let's have lunch before I make tracks." Esther commented.

"I had noticed that you don't stay all day."

"I somehow thought that would be excessive. It also gives Zack some time with the children in the afternoon."

"Ethan has started taking the afternoon off as well."

"Good thing they are self employed."

"True. What happened to the model agency?"

"I terminated their contract, when I discovered them doing nude photo shoots."

"Really, where was I?"

"About to have your children." Esther replied.

17

"Sorry, I meant to be finished at 1.00." Ethan said coming into the lounge later.

"I was about to feed the children. You look a bit flustered."

"Not flustered, more like flabbergasted."

"How come?"

"Let's get this lot fed and I'll tell you."

"Okay."

"Wow, they are getting bigger." Ethan said several hours later, plopping on the couch.

"That tends to happen when one feeds them."

"Yeah, I know. They are also starting to develop their own personalities."

"That tends to happen as well." Estelle said, giving him a soft punch on the arm.

"Ouch!" Ethan said with exaggeration.

"Oh, you goof. By the way, seeing I was out cold when they were born. Who came first?"

"Let me think. Um, Devyn, then Kezia, and Xavier."

"We will have to try and make sure that none of them is lost in the crowd, so to speak."

"I've noticed that Xavier, can be bossy. Kezia boisterous, and Devyn booming."

"Maybe we should have given them names that began with B, but that's not the sort of thing I mean."

"Personally, I think they are still sorting out who is who, amongst themselves, let alone anyone else." Ethan commented.

"You could be right about that."

"Did you ask Esther?"

"Yes, she rang Kylie, and I have an appointment on Wednesday. She is going to come with me."

"Good. I might be a bit busy."

"Does this have anything to do with what you want to tell me?"

"Yes. But you have to be a little patient as I'm still processing it."

"I'll try."

"Believe me when I tell you it is worth the wait."

"Now I intrigued."

"Who is going to look after the children for that day?"

"Esther rang Gina, and she seemed quite pleased. She's probably rung the others."

"I don't think she will have any trouble roping in Richard. He'll be staying for a week or so."

"I almost forgot that he'll be here."

"He loves spending time with all five of them." Ethan remarked.

"How he does it, I'm not sure. He always seems to be busy."

"Do you know what he does?" Ethan asked.

"I know he was doing an engineering job and wasn't happy and left recently."

"Do you know why he left?"

"I didn't even think to ask."

"Well, I did. You might be surprised at what has been happening in his life."

"Don't keep me in suspense." Estelle said.

"First, the reason he is staying in the mobile home has to do with a job interview."

"Really!"

"I'm not sure you're going to believe this."

"Try me."

"Owning and operating a childcare centre. It seems that he has done a course for the last couple of years. He has also been seeing a lot of a certain lady called Fleur. He met her through the course. Apparently, she works at a centre. There's probably a wedding in their future."

"I'm gobsmacked."

"Told you. That's not all of it. They are thinking of either taking over the centre where Fleur works or even building their own."

"Wow."

"Right, now to tell you my news."

"I think I'm ready. Still processing about Richard."

"Fair enough. Want me to wait before I tell you?"

"No way. Don't you dare?" Estelle said, giving another playful punch.

"Enough of the punching already." Ethan said, rubbing his arm. "Right, I was approached by a person involved in building a well known hotel chain. He has seen my work and wants me to build units to go into these hotels."

"Wow."

"He has taken some photos, which he can add to their advertising."

"Does that mean more work?"

"Not really. I explained my work schedule, about the children, as well as our monthly weekend away."

"And?"

"He is more than happy to work in with what I want. And I do still have the offer of help of apprentices, or even help from some of his men."

"I think that we have both earned this particular weekend away."

"I also contacted all the people involved with the bible study."

"Why?"

"To let them know that the group might be on hold for a while."

"Thanks for just assuming that I wouldn't be able to handle that."

"Tell me something. When was the last time we held it?"

"When I was pregnant."

"You would have noticed that not everyone attended."

"So," Estelle sighed.

"I didn't want to put too pressure or even add the burden of organising the children to be in bed earlier."

"Every so often is not going to hurt them. I enjoy those. I even get up early so that I get at least half an hour time with the Lord."

"Do you want to go back to doing it together?"

"Possibly."

"You know, of course, that you don't have a specific place or time to be able to pray or have time with the Lord." Ethan remarked.

"How dare do you suggest I don't know how to organise my time. Until recently, when I had the children, my time was well organised. Now, don't get me wrong, I'm not going to put any blame on the children, and I don't regret for one moment having them."

"I wasn't suggesting for a moment that you don't know how to organise your time." Ethan said, taking a breath. "I'm fully aware of how tiring it has been for the both of us."

"And I don't think that it is going to get easier as they get older." Estelle commented.

"You could be right about that. So, what do you think we should do about that?"

"I'm not sure." Estelle said running her hands through her hair. "The weekends and spa days are helping me. But what about you?"

"I manage to get a break after breakfast."

"Is it enough?"

"Yes. Would you like to employ a nanny on either a full time or part time basis?"Ethan asked.

"I believe that God has entrusted us with these three, and I don't think we should rely too much on a nanny. Beside we do have the family helping."

"We might have to call a meeting and see if they are happy with the arrangements."

"They have their lives as well, and that's what concerns me a little. I mean they might have put off all sorts of things that they had planned."

"I think that you may be putting obstacles where they might not be."

"What about Layla and Bryce? Or even Richard and Fleur?"

"How did Bryce and Fleur get into this?" Ethan asked.

"They could be future partners of Layla and Richard."

"Don't forget any future partners for Samuel, or even Felicity."

"Now, you're being ridiculous."

"You are the one that started down this particular track. And what is so ridiculous about any of them marrying?"

"I didn't mean that it couldn't happen."

"Okay, let's both calm down. How about we call a meeting and go from there."

"The sooner the better."

"How about Tuesday or Wednesday next week?"

"Okay."

"I'll ring Gina and Layla."

"Why those two?" Estelle asked.

"Even if they are adoptive mothers, they are still our mothers."

"True."

"I'm heading back to the workshop for a while. This will give us both times to calm down. I'll also ring Gina and Layla."

"Now, don't shoot the messenger. It seems that the meeting will have to wait." Ethan said later on.

"How long?"

"Maybe two months or more."

"See what I mean about putting their lives on hold."

"That doesn't mean that the meeting won't happen. Both Gina and Layla thought it was a good idea to delay it." Ethan replied.

"Why?"

"So that you can have several counselling sessions under your belt so to speak."

"So, they all know about those."

"Yes, do you have a problem with them knowing?"

"Yes. No. Sort of. I don't really know how I feel right at this moment."

"You're not pregnant, by any chance?"

"When have we had time for that sort of intimacy?"

"You're right. But you know, of course, that sort of intimacy as you call doesn't have to be confined to night-time."

18

"I see that your children are just about ready for their rest too." Esther commented, as she and Zack came into the room, on the day of the meeting six months later.

"And our two shouldn't disturb them too much." Zack added.

"No. And don't worry about those voices you can hear, downstairs. I organised Layla and Gina to arrive early so that we could settle this lot." Ethan remarked.

"They are more active at ten months old." Estelle remarked.

"Yeah. I have been thinking about a baby gate for downstairs, as they are starting to crawl." Ethan replied.

"Good thinking. Even though our two are not at that stage, it won't be long." Esther commented.

"More than one baby gate." Estelle suggested.

"Okay, we can sort that out later. I think we should join that lot downstairs." Ethan commented.

"Did you know that all these people were involved?" Estelle asked, looking at Ethan, as she had looked at each of the other six people, including Zack and Esther in the room.

"No."

"We had no idea either." Zack commented.

"And a few that help, are not here at the moment." Gina remarked.

"Who else is there?"

"Samuel, Richard, Fleur, and Bryce." Paul replied.

"Okay, this is all doing my head in." Estelle commented.

"We were hoping that the counselling sessions were helping." Gina said.

"They are. This is just a little overwhelming for me right now."

"Where did my confident, outgoing little girl go?" Gina asked.

"Not sure. I think that she's still there."

"You know, of course, that it is okay to have help, and have it on a regular basis." Felicity remarked.

"Yes, but it doesn't really take the guilt away."

"What guilt?" Layla asked.

"The fact that you're putting all your lives on hold."

"Explain." Gina said.

"Well, there could be some weddings coming up."

"You're right about that. But I don't see what that has to do with us."

"I'm finding that hard to explain."

"Does it have anything to do with being a parent?" Felicity asked.

"Sort of."

"Can I ask you some questions Estelle?" Layla asked.

"Go ahead." Estelle said. "It seems to be pick on Estelle day"

"That statement is so, not true. We are all here to help." Gina stated.

"I don't want you to misconstrue, what I'm about to say in any way possible. Okay. No need to answer that. I've been sitting here, praying. Yes, I'm a Christian. I asked the Lord to show me the possible cause of all your insecurities. Do you trust us?"

"Of course."

"All of us in this room are parents, right?"

"Yes."

"To your way of thinking, we have all made it look easy."

"Yes."

"Have you ever asked any of us, what help we had with our children?" Layla asked.

"No." Estelle replied sheepishly.

"I only had one person." Layla added.

"I had three people that I could call." Gina said.

"Five people." Felicity said.

"Three." John and Faye remarked together.

"Now I feel extra spoilt with all these people helping raise my two." Esther commented.

"I want to say that I for one wouldn't be here if I didn't want to be here." Layla said.

"Neither would we." Paul, Faye, Felicity, John, chorused together.

"I love that as a grandparent, I get to spend some time with them." Felicity added.

"Not quite sure whether I'm classed as a grandparent, but I still love that time I have." Faye said.

"What do you mean, about not being classed as a grandparent?" Ethan asked.

"What with all that happened." Faye said.

"Before you go any further. You did your best, and even got beaten up. You even supplied us with bodyguards and sat by my bed, while I was in a coma. You're Felicity's sister, therefore you're an Aunt. I for one think of you as a grandparent." Estelle said.

"Thanks for clarifying that." Faye said.

"Estelle is the only one that could have said that." Ethan said. "And I for one agree. To me, you're a grandparent."

"Here's another question. Do you have any issues with the children's safety; say in the last six months?" Layla asked.

"No. I think I was more concerned about what they might be thinking etc."

"Don't you think that at one time or another we haven't had the same thoughts about our children." Gina asked.

"Yes."

"Even when those children are grown." Felicity added.

"So, these thoughts are normal?" Estelle asked.

"Perfectly. Being a parent is a twenty four hour, seven days a week job."

"That is not exactly helpful." Estelle remarked.

"The one thing about being a grandparent is that we get to hand them back." Gina added.

"That's not helpful either."

"How many sessions have you had with the counsellor?" Paul asked.

"Seven." Estelle replied.

"Any idea how many you have to go?"

"No."

"Have you even asked?" Esther asked.

"No."Estelle replied sheepishly.

"I have an idea. Why don't we have a review every six months or so and then if there is something that is coming up for one of us, we can all be part of the planning."Paul said.

"What if it's a wedding? I would like the children involved."

"Your point being?" Layla asked.

"Most of the adults will be involved, right."

"Yes but doesn't mean we can't hire a couple of people, to help with the children for the day."

"I hadn't thought about that."

"Now that we have solved that I think we can get on with life." Gina said.

"You know, of course, that being a Christian doesn't guarantee a smooth or trouble free life?" Faye asked.

"Are all of you Christians?" Estelle asked.

"Yes. Most of us for years, but one or two newer ones." Faye replied.

"Okay. Okay. I think that I need to talk to my doctor about getting something to relax me a bit."

"Good thinking." Ethan remarked.

"I think I can hear someone stirring."John remarked.

"Let's bring them all down here."

"Good idea. There are more than enough people here to help." Esther commented.

"Why don't we get organised and go down to the park?" Faye asked.

"I like." Estelle replied.

"This is nice."Estelle said, from one of three blanket set up, three hours later.

"Thought you might like it." Gina said.

"As you can see, all of the children seem quite happy not to go very far." Paul remarked.

"What about when they start crawling or even walking?" Estelle asked.

"We will think of something." Zack said.

"They do have to crawl before they can walk." Esther said.

"How are Ethan and I going to manage on our own?" Estelle asked.

"There are plenty of willing helpers right here." Gina said.

"True. So, I can ring any one of you the morning I decide that I want to bring them here in the afternoon."

"That could work." Paul replied.

"Now, there is one thing we have been wondering about?" John remarked.

"And what might that be?" Ethan asked.

"What they should call us." Layla said.

"It seems only right that they respect all of you as their grandparents." Estelle replied.

"I agree with that." Zack said.

"Just to clarify they are not allowed to call us Paul, Gina, etc."

"Definitely not." Ethan replied.

"There does need to be some consistency with who is called what." Esther remarked.

"I agree with that." Zack said. "Can't call Layla, Nanna, at our house and Grandma's at Ethan and Estelle's."

"Got any preferences?" Ethan asked.

"Grandma." Layla replied.

"Nanna." Gina said.

"Pops." John said.

"Nanna," Faye said.

"Nanna," Felicity said.

"Could get a bit confusing with too many Nannas." Esther remarked.

"They could always call Faye by the name we had for our Grandma." Felicity commented.

"True." Faye replied. "We called her GM."

"Right all sorted. One Grandma, two Nannas one GM and one Pops." Esther said.

"You haven't said what you would prefer, Dad?" Estelle said.

"I'm trying to decide between Poppy or Papa."

"I like Poppy." Esther commented. "Not that I even get a say."

"What do you mean?" Estelle asked quizzically.

"He's your adoptive father not mine."

"True. How our family is blended is a little unusual."

"Hey, I'm right here." Paul said. "I like Poppy too. And for your clarification Esther, you are my daughter."

"See." Estelle said, giving Esther a punch on the arm. "I suggest that we start making tracks for home, as it is getting near teatime."

"Okay miss bossy boots." Esther said.

"Someone has to take charge."

"So, you nominated yourself."

"Why not?"

"Tea at our place?" Ethan asked, standing between Estelle and Esther.

"If their mothers are anything to go by. It'll be interesting watching their children grow." Felicity commented.

"Esther and I wouldn't have really come to blows."

"Could have fooled me." Zack said.

"I'm actually meeting Bryce, so will have to bow out." Layla said.

"If we promise to behave, will you call him and ask him to join us?"

"Possibly." Layla replied.

"I'll behave, when a certain little sister, apologises." Esther commented.

"Apologise for what?"

"For assuming that I'll behave."

"They both have that stubborn look." Gina said.

"We know that look, don't we Faye." Felicity said.

"We sure do. This could last for hours. Let's get this lot home and leave them here." Faye said.

"Okay, okay, I apologise."

"Good. Because my stubbornness was starting to dissolve."

"Mine too." Estelle said, putting an arm around Esther's shoulder. "Let's leave this lot here."

"We can't really do that. Some of them are our children."

"That's true."Estelle replied. "We could grab one of our children each and make a run for it."

"That won't work either."

"Why not?"

"You'd probably take forever to decide which one of your three to grab."

"You know me too well."

"There's the confident, outgoing girl, I know." Gina remarked.

"And the one I married." Ethan commented.

"I didn't realise how much I had isolated myself by staying at home." Estelle replied.

"Some of that has to do with raising the children." Paul remarked.

"True. Being outside has sure chased some of the blues away."

"It is amazing what a bit of fresh air can do." Ethan commented.

"Why don't we try and do it weekly?" Esther suggested.

"That would be nice, but how?" Estelle said, looking quizzical.

"You know it is plausible." Ethan commented.

"If we aim for an afternoon." Esther remarked.

"That way, Ethan and I could help." Zack added.

"Do we want to set it for the same afternoon each week?"Estelle asked.

"Let's try for Wednesday afternoon next week and go from there." Zack suggested.

"Sounds like a good idea." Esther commented.

"I like. Okay, let's round up the troops and head back." Estelle said.

The End.